"You're not alone. We'll help each other through this."

She wanted to riot against him, to push him away and deny his reasonableness. But it felt too good to lean on someone for a change. Someone with a hard chest and muscular arms, who smelled like a dream and warmed her with the heat of his body. Giving in, she laid her head on his shoulder and closed her eyes so he couldn't see her anguish.

"I don't want to like you."

His chest rumbled under her ear when he laughed, and he stroked her hair the way she stroked little Cody when she held him.

The tender caress both soothed and unnerved.

Dear Reader,

My sister has a set of twin girls (along with five more girls), and though double the loving, the twins were also double the trouble. So what better way to bring two strangers together than to have them care for two orphaned babies?

Love and duty collide as a small-town loner goes up against a world traveler with an extensive family. The instant parents soon learn that ten-month-olds, like animals, can sense fear. Humor and unity help get them through. The common ground is an unexpected, inconvenient attraction that complicates the question of custody!

I had great fun writing about twins. It was a learning experience, though. When I was plotting my story I asked my sister with the seven girls if she thought it was believable for a parent to bequeath guardianship of their children without ever advising the guardian. Not only did she agree it was, she grinned evilly and confessed she was glad to hear I felt that way, too. Oh, boy, am I praying for her continued good health!

Best wishes,

Teresa

TERESA CARPENTER

Baby Twins: Parents Needed

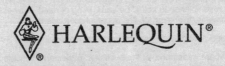

TORONTO • NEW YORK • LONDON
AMSTERDAM • PARIS • SYDNEY • HAMBURG
STOCKHOLM • ATHENS • TOKYO • MILAN • MADRID
PRAGUE • WARSAW • BUDAPEST • AUCKLAND

ISBN-13: 978-0-373-03971-5
ISBN-10:   0-373-03971-9

BABY TWINS: PARENTS NEEDED

First North American Publication 2007.

Copyright © 2007 by Teresa Carpenter.

This edition published by arrangement with Harlequin Books S.A.

® and TM are trademarks of the publisher. Trademarks indicated with ® are registered in the United States Patent and Trademark Office, the Canadian Trade Marks Office and in other countries.

www.eHarlequin.com

Printed in U.S.A.

Teresa Carpenter believes in the power of unconditional love, and that there's no better place to find it than between the pages of a romance novel. Reading is a passion for Teresa—a passion that led to a calling. She began writing more than twenty years ago, and marks the sale of her first book as one of her happiest memories. Teresa gives back to her craft by volunteering her time to Romance Writers of America on a local and national level. A fifth-generation Californian, she lives in San Diego within miles of her extensive family, and knows that with their help she can accomplish anything. She takes particular joy and pride in her nieces and nephews, who are all bright, fit, shining stars of the future. If she's not at a family event you'll usually find her at home, reading, writing or playing with her adopted Chihuahua, Jefe.

To Jill Limber, critique partner, writing buddy
and lunch companion, I'm lucky to have you
in my corner. And to Michelle and Gabrielle,
my favorite twins in the whole wide world.

CHAPTER ONE

RACHEL ADAMS was at war. And the enemy outnumbered her two to one. Hands on her hips she surveyed two plump-cheeked, hazel-eyed cherubs smeared head to foot in baby lotion.

"Cody Anthony Adams," Rachel admonished the unrepentant ten-month-old, "if you can't keep your hands to yourself, I'm going to duct tape them to your diaper during your naps."

The sight of the greasy mess acted like scissors to nerves already frayed thin by exhaustion. Inhaling a calming breath, she reminded herself she was a mother now. That it had happened by default didn't matter. She'd made a vow to provide a home for her orphaned niece and nephew.

But boy did she have a lot to learn.

Already she'd discovered that children, like animals, sensed fear.

God knows she'd had little time to mourn the sister she'd barely known. Instead, Rachel had learned that messes happened. Literally. And repeatedly. And if she didn't keep things far enough out of Cody's reach, creatively. Usually with food, jelly, bananas, potatoes whatever he could get into when she turned her back. He liked to finger paint. And his favorite target was his sister.

Yuck, yuck, yuck.

Armed with rubber gloves and a tub of wet wipes she went on the attack, cleaning bodies, fingers and toes. And hair. Both babies needed a bath to complete the job. She made a mental note to move the crib another six inches from the changing table.

It struck her suddenly; this must be love. When forbearance overshadowed disgust and exasperation, letting affection rule, there could be no other explanation.

Sometime over the last six days she'd fallen in love. And it was huge, bigger than anything she'd ever experienced.

The feeling terrified her.

One thing was for sure, if her co-guardian ever deigned to show his face, she'd fight with everything she had to keep her niece and nephew.

"That's right, kiddos, you're stuck with me. I'm wholeheartedly, irrevocably a goner. And I'm keeping you. I promise that you will always know you are loved. You'll never have to worry about simply being tolerated or that you're here only because of a sense of duty.

"We're a family now," she whispered around the lump in her throat.

Stripping off the rubber gloves, Rachel ran her fingers through the slick darkness of Cody's hair. She kept looking for signs of her sister in the twins, and caught the occasional expression. But they must have gotten their dark hair and eyes from their father, because Crystal had brown eyes and light brown hair.

Crystal had gotten her coloring from her father. Rachel took after their mother with white-blond hair that she kept short and manageable and eyes that couldn't decide if they were blue or green.

A sudden knock at the front door interrupted her musings.

Rachel tensed. "Who could that be?"

Wearily blowing a strand of hair from her eyes, she looked at the naked babies and considered ignoring the door. Whoever it was couldn't have come at a worse time.

Jolie began to cry. In the week the twins had been in her care, Rachel had learned that Cody liked to be naked but Jolie didn't.

A loner who preferred animals and plants to most people, Rachel didn't usually get visitors; not even her neighbors. But whoever banged on her door meant business, pounding again almost immediately.

Leaving the twins in the safety of the crib, making sure nothing else was within Cody's reach, Rachel made her way to the door reminding herself she wasn't a loner anymore. Through the peephole she saw a man half-turned away from her with hands tucked into the pockets of his dark jacket.

Hmm. Could this be Ford Sullivan, co-guardian of the twins? A Navy SEAL, his commanding officer had explained that Sullivan, aka Mustang, was out of the country when the twins were orphaned but he would be in touch as soon as he returned from assignment.

As far as she was concerned he could stay away.

She opened the door a few inches.

The man appeared bigger and broader than his image through the peephole. Much bigger. Much broader. Dressed in jeans and leather with dark glasses, biker boots and a five-o'clock shadow as accessories, his stance warned he wasn't someone to mess with. Snow fell from a gray sky, landing in white clusters on wide shoulders and dark hair.

This man bypassed bad and went straight to dangerous.

A sucker for a good action movie, the sight of this tall, dark and menacing man sent unexpected, and unwanted, tingles down the back of Rachel's neck.

She crossed her fingers he was a motorist who'd run out of gas.

"Yes?" she said. She purposely did not ask if she could help him. Or smile. She'd found smiling only encouraged people to linger when most of the time she preferred her own company.

"Rachel Adams?" he asked. His deep baritone slid as smoothly as hot coffee through the icy afternoon air.

And just as smoothly and potently down her spine.

"Yes." She shifted restlessly, thinking in the back of her mind that she needed to put her SUV in the barn.

"Your sister was Crystal Adams?"

So much for him being an anonymous motorist. Her head went back, and she narrowed her gaze on him. "Ford Sullivan I presume?"

He cocked his head in acknowledgment. "Yes. I've come to collect the twins."

Hackles bristling, Rachel planted her hand dead

center of his chest when the military man attempted to cross her threshold.

"Hold it, big guy. I don't know you. And so far, I don't like what I'm hearing."

Sullivan didn't give an inch, but his eyes narrowed and she felt the flex of muscle under her fingers, silent warnings of strength and resolution. He reached inside his jacket and came out with a wallet. He handed her his military ID.

She knew of Navy SEALS. They were elite, Special Forces who were dropped into hot spots all over the world. Granted, her knowledge came from movies and books, but there was no denying it rated as very high security stuff.

After a moment, he plucked his ID from her chilled fingertips. "Lady I've driven a long way, and it's cold out here."

Damn him. She didn't want him in her home, not when he talked about taking the twins away. Not when she wanted to keep the twins herself. But he had legal rights she couldn't ignore.

Reluctantly she stood aside and let him come inside. His commanding officer had said Sullivan was an honorable man. Right. His edges were so rough he practically chafed her skin as he stepped past her.

Blowing out a pent-up breath, she closed the door. Then clenched her teeth against the sight of him framed by the hearth fire. His big body made her blue and gray living room seem entirely too small.

And more disorderly than she'd realized. The babies came with a lot of clutter, and a lot of demands.

Picking up was a luxury that came right after sleeping and showering.

Jolie's cries from the bedroom reminded Rachel where she'd left off. Grim amusement lifted the corner of her mouth. She'd just been thinking she was at war and here stood a warrior.

He wanted the babies? She knew just how he could help.

"I'm so glad you're here." Pretending not to see the disdain with which Sullivan viewed her home, she hooked her arm through his and drew him into the bedroom. "Because the twins need a bath."

To his credit Sullivan didn't flinch. He took off his sunglasses revealing sharp blue, expressionless eyes. He tossed the glasses along with his leather jacket onto the bed.

Jolie immediately stopped crying to stare at Sullivan. Rachel didn't blame her. Soft black cotton defined muscular shoulders and hard pecks. His arms were strong and browned by the sun. He heated the room better than a fireplace.

Something she shouldn't be noticing. Still, she empathized when she cleaned the drool from Jolie's chin.

"What happened?" he asked as he stepped up to the crib.

Rachel took perverse pleasure in explaining Cody's little habit.

He hiked a dark brow. "You might want to check on them more often."

"Wow, why didn't I think of that?" Jerk. She lifted Jolie into her arms. "Grab Cody. The bathroom's through here."

Rachel flinched at the sight of dirty towels and over-flowing clothes and wastebaskets. Half the contents of her medicine cabinet littered the sink. And—she cringed—was that a fork?

Ignoring the mess, and the rush of embarrassment, she bent to start the bathwater. Once it ran warm she set the stopper and knelt on a towel still folded next to the tub from the babies' last bath. Then she set Jolie in the warm water.

Sullivan knelt next to her, so close his arm brushed her shoulder as he lowered Cody into the water. Rachel jumped away as if singed by steam.

She shot to her feet. "Watch the babies, I'll grab clean towels."

"Clean would be good," he said, making no attempt to hide the derision.

Stunned she swung around to confront him, but his attention remained on the twins. She waffled for several seconds on whether to appease or challenge him on his concerns regarding the condition of the house.

On the one hand, the house was a mess; on the other, she'd been handling their wards on her own for six days. How dare he judge her?

She'd like to see him do better.

No, she turned away to get the towels, that wasn't true. That would mean he'd have the twins and she needed to care for them, to be there for them, because she hadn't been there for her sister.

If he thought she'd simply step aside and allow him to take them away, he could forget it.

"How did you know Crystal?" she asked as she returned to the tub.

Making sure to leave plenty of room between her and Sullivan, she knelt next to him. She glanced at him, then away, pretending not to notice how the twins' excited play had dampened his T-shirt causing the fabric to cling to his impressive chest.

"Eeey!" Cody shrieked in joy and slapped the water with both hands, splashing everyone. Jolie shied away, the movement causing her to slide sideways. Rachel reached for her, but Sullivan got there first, catching Jolie in his large, competent hands.

He held her with such gentleness, righting her and making her giggle. He appeared so calm despite his obvious frustration with the circumstances.

"It wasn't Crystal I knew." He finally answered her question as he scrubbed Jolie's tummy. "At least not well. Tony Valenti was my friend. We worked together."

"The twins' father?"

"Yeah."

"He was a SEAL, too?"

"Yeah." A short pause. "He saved my life."

"I see." Yeah, she did. And the picture didn't look good. An honorable man, he'd feel all the more obligated to take the twins because of what he felt he owed his dead friend.

An hour later the babies had been bathed, dressed and fed. Lowering Jolie into the playpen and tossing in a few plastic blocks, Rachel had to admit having an extra pair of hands had made everything easier. And faster. It would have taken her nearly twice as long to complete the tasks on her own.

She turned to where Sullivan sat on the sofa with Cody. The little boy looked up at him and smiled showing two bottom teeth. The man ran a gentle finger down the baby's cheek then bounced him on his knee.

Cody reached up and grabbed a handful of dark hair. Sullivan calmly freed himself.

They'd bonded quickly.

She crossed her arms over her chest, denying that his tenderness toward the baby touched her. She walked to the opposite end of the sofa and began folding the clean clothes mounded in the corner.

"What are your plans for the twins?" she demanded.

He lifted a dark brow at her directness. "I plan to honor my friend's request by taking them back to San Diego to raise them."

Her heart clenched as he confirmed her worst fear. "Right. And what about me?"

"Simple. I plan for you to sign over your custody."

"Simple?" She nearly choked on the word. "How can you hold that baby in your arms and call this simple?"

He frowned, shifting the baby. Cody tipped back his head and looked up at the expanse of black fabric, to the man's face. Silent communication passed between them as once again, Sullivan pulled the baby's fist from his hair.

Sullivan focused his blue gaze on her. "I understand this isn't easy for you. But it's for the best."

"You don't understand anything, Sullivan. I failed my sister once. I'm not going to fail her now. Her dying wish was that I raise her children. And that's what I'm going to do."

He eyed her for a moment before cocking his head

in acknowledgment. "Your sister never intended for you to raise her children."

Rachel's head went up and back as if she'd taken a blow to the chin. It couldn't have hurt more if Sullivan had actually hit her.

Old guilt rose up to choke her. Resolutely she shook it off. She and Crystal had put the past behind them when their parents died three years ago and Crystal had come to stay with Rachel. And when Crystal had left for San Diego State University, they'd stayed in touch by phone and e-mail.

Rachel was the only family Crystal had had left in the world. Through all of her uncertainty and exhaustion this last week, Rachel had held on to the fact that her sister had trusted her to take care of Jolie and Cody.

She caught herself rubbing her arms as if to ward off a chill. When she felt Sullivan watching her, she clenched her hands into fists and dropped them to her sides.

"Why would you say something so hateful?" Rachel demanded.

"Look I only know what Tony told me. Crystal didn't like it that Tony made a will naming a guardian for the twins without consulting her. So she made her own will and named you as guardian."

"Which just proves she wanted me to raise her children." Something deep inside her eased.

"No, you were leverage. No offense, but Tony didn't want someone who ran away from life and responsibilities, who couldn't maintain a relationship to raise his kids."

Everything in Rachel screamed a denial of his claim, of this whole situation. But it was here; *he* was here, standing in her living room and not budging by the look of it.

"I don't believe you." Believe? Not likely. "If this is a joke, it's in very poor taste."

"No joke." He hesitated, and she could practically hear the debate going on internally. Being free with information obviously wasn't part of his job description. "That would be cruel. Listen, I have a large, close-knit family that Tony was a part of. He wanted the twins to have that connection."

Sullivan bent to retrieve his jacket and withdraw some papers. He extended them to Rachel. "I have legal documents here for you to sign over custody."

She reluctantly lowered her gaze from him to the folded papers he offered. She didn't want to take them, didn't want to think he spoke the truth about her sister's motives. But she'd learned long ago no good came from lying to herself.

Or from avoiding reality.

He looked around the cluttered room then met her gaze. "Clearly you're out of your depth."

"That's ridiculous." She ignored the proffered papers to pick up a tiny set of overalls, folding them over and over. "I'm not overwhelmed. I just need time to adjust."

He rose and settled Cody next to Jolie in the playpen. "And while you adjust, the twins suffer."

Anger, simmering under the surface since she opened the door to this ungrateful man, rose to a boil. She planted her hands on her hips and glared in outrage.

"How dare you? They have not suffered. So I'm behind in my housekeeping. So what? You caught me on a bad day. I usually pick up when they're in bed, but last night I had to write. I had a deadline."

He gestured to the cluttered room, his blue eyes flashing with impatience. "This is more than one day's filth. Make this easy on both of us. Sign over custody to me and you won't have to adjust and you won't have to pick up after them any longer."

"Okay, that's it!" Rachel had had enough. Filth? Oh, she'd had more than enough.

Stomping into her room she grabbed up the diaper bag. A quick glance inventoried the contents. Going to the changing table she stuffed in more diapers, two sleepers, a pack of wipes, some formula.

"You think you can do better?" She marched by Sullivan on her way to the kitchen.

"I think you need to calm down." Sullivan watched her efforts with an impassive expression that only fueled her anger.

She ripped open the refrigerator door, hissing when her thumbnail caught in the handle and tore. Tears rushed forward, but she blinked them away determined to show no weakness in front of the cold man watching—and judging—her every move.

"Oh, I'm calm." She quickly tore off the broken nail and stuffed her finger in her mouth as she held the door open with her hip and plucked two bottles from the refrigerator adding them to the other items in the red baby bag.

Glaring at her nemesis, she stepped up to him and thrust the overflowing bag into his arms. She half hoped he'd drop it, but he quickly controlled the bag.

"I'm just wonderful."

Adrenaline pumping through her, she brushed past him on her way to the playpen where she swooped Jolie up into her arms. From the edge of the playpen Rachel snagged two blankets. Folding one around Jolie, Rachel tossed the other to Sullivan who now eyed her with sharp-eyed wariness.

"Bring Cody."

"What's happening here, Rachel?"

"I'm doing you a favor." Finding her coat, she pulled her car keys from the pocket and headed for the door.

"You're going to sign the papers?"

A bitter laugh broke free. "Better than that. I'm not signing the papers."

He caught up with her at her Toyota SUV and swung her and Jolie to face him. "Where do you think you're going?"

She shook him off. "I'm not going anywhere. You are." She took the diaper bag from him, opened the front door and tossed it inside. "You wanted the twins? You've got them. For the next twenty-four hours."

"Excuse me?" Now his tone held a bite. "I'm not accustomed to taking orders."

"Yes, you are, you're in the Navy."

Let him argue that.

His expression didn't change; he was too much a warrior to give anything away that easily. But his shoulders went up and back, fighting ready. A clear indication she'd hit a nerve.

She should be ashamed of the satisfaction that gave her, but he threatened her on too many levels.

"You seem to think two babies are so easy to care

for." Walking around him, she opened the door, put Jolie in her car seat and began to belt her in. "Right. Fine. You're going to get your chance."

Sullivan had left the door open. Cody didn't care to be left alone in the house, and he made his displeasure heard with loud cries. Flashing Sullivan a disdainful glare, she suggested, "You might want to start by getting Cody."

"Not until I understand what's going on here." Before her eyes he changed from civilian to warrior. His hands lowered to his sides, his chin jutted down and his blue eyes chilled by several degrees.

Climbing from the car, she closed the door with soft emphasis. She instinctively kept her distance, out of reach of his sensual appeal. What was with her that this stranger's dangerous edge affected her so easily?

"The first thing you have to learn is you don't get to take the high road when a baby is crying."

He spiked a hand through his dark hair. "You're right." Turning he loped into the house and came back out a few moments later with his jacket under his arm and Cody wrapped in a blanket.

Okay, so Sullivan got points for common sense.

She reached for Cody, but Sullivan held him fast. She lifted one eyebrow and waited.

"We need to talk first," he stated.

"No, we'll talk after." Facing him, she propped hands on hips. "After you've tried to feed and change two babies. After you've spent a sleepless night trying to get them both to sleep at the same time. After you haven't brushed your teeth before noon and your best shirt's stained beyond repair. Then we'll talk."

The sound of grinding teeth reached her across the two feet separating them. He shook his head. "What's to stop me from taking them and driving on to San Diego?"

She narrowed her eyes at him, and this time when she reached for Cody she refused to be cowed.

"Honor. Integrity. I spoke to your commanding officer. He assured me you have both in spades." She walked around the SUV and set Cody in his car seat. Kissing his dark curls, she tucked the blanket around him.

Bending, she gathered a few scattered toys and handed one to each baby. They immediately tried to take a bite. Her heart turned over. How trusting they were. At ten months old life wasn't that complicated.

"I'm doing this for you guys." She told them. "Have no mercy."

She rounded the SUV to rejoin Sullivan.

"Plus, I haven't signed the papers." She held out her hand, palm up. "Keys."

"I thought you meant for me to take them." None of the tension had left those truly impressive shoulders.

"To your Jeep. You're taking my vehicle, I'll need to keep yours."

Silence stretched while she met those compelling blue eyes head-on. The scowl creasing his brow revealed his displeasure at the situation.

"Look, I'm not giving these babies up without a fight, but I'm exhausted, dirty and hungry. In no shape to have an important discussion. And until you've spent some quality time with the twins, you're in no shape for the discussion, either. So we trade keys and regroup tomorrow."

He hesitated for a heartbeat.

Time slowed. Breath misted on the air. Her nerves jumped.

Finally he handed over his keys and took hers in exchange.

"I hope you realize what you're doing," he said as he climbed inside the vehicle and adjusted the seat. "Honor and integrity don't make me a gentleman." He closed the door and turned over the ignition, rolling down the window a crack. "I'm a SEAL. And we never leave a man behind."

Rachel watched the taillights disappear down the driveway, praying she hadn't just made the biggest mistake of her life.

CHAPTER TWO

FORD pulled into a slot in front of his hotel room, slowly turned the ignition off, eased back in his seat and closed his eyes. Twenty hours after leaving Rachel Adams's house and he was ready to run back to her door with head and tail tucked low.

How humiliating.

Using all the stealth learned over eight years in the SEALS; he risked moving to check on the babies in the back seat. Jolie, as tidy and neat as when he'd strapped her in, slept with her pink beanie on her head and her bottle nestled close. Cody, who'd long ago lost his hat and shoes, had a catsup smear on his cheek and a French fry clutched in his fist.

They'd finally fallen asleep an hour ago.

Ford settled back in his seat. He planned to sit right where he was for as long as they slept.

Time well spent finding an appetizing way to eat crow. Only sheer stubborn will had kept him from running back to Rachel's place hours ago. How had she managed on her own for six days?

A call home netted him lots of advice from Gram, and other family and friends, but the twins were having none of it. Nothing he'd done, or said, or sung—yes he'd sung to them—had done any good. Talk about logistical nightmares, he'd rather plan a two-team infiltration any day than repeat the last twenty hours.

Clearly they wanted Rachel.

Hell, he wanted Rachel, and it had nothing to do with the soft curves hidden under her burp-stained sweater. Okay, that was a lie. No man could look at her trim little figure and remain unaffected. But her sweet butt and perky bosom were beside the point. He'd misjudged her big time. For six days she'd cared for the two babies with patience and devotion.

He knew that because they were clean, well fed and distraught without her.

With one or the other, or both, of the babies awake most of the night; he'd gotten about two hours sleep. And she'd had them for six nights. No wonder her pretty sea-green eyes had dark bruises shadowing them.

She was one feisty woman. A blond wildcat determined to stand between him and her cubs. But for all her attitude, she was a lightweight. Barely five foot five, six at the most, her sweet curves scarcely filled out her jeans or rounded out her gold sweater.

Obviously she'd been ignoring herself to care for the twins. Protective instincts had flared when he should have been thinking of ways to convince her the babies were better off with him.

He'd told her a SEAL never left a man behind, which was nothing less than the truth. He could no more leave

Tony's twins in the care of another than he could leave a teammate on the battlefield.

He tensed and turned to the window just before the local sheriff rapped on the glass. He held up a hand and eased from the car.

"Officer." Ford addressed the man who looked like Mr. Clean in a uniform. Sheriff Mitchell according to his badge. "What can I do for you?"

"Sir." The sheriff crossed his arms over his massive chest and nodded toward Rachel's SUV. "Problem?"

"No." Ford made sure to keep his hands in plain view as he leaned against the SUV, not wanting the officer to feel threatened. Had the hotel owner called the law? He'd been to Ford's room twice in response to complaints about the babies' crying. "No problem."

The last thing he had time for was trouble from the local law enforcement.

"This is Rachel Adams's vehicle." Sheriff Mitchell took two steps to the side and looked into the back seat. "Those are her wards."

"Yes." What game was Rachel playing? Did she regret sending him away with the twins? "Has she called with a complaint?"

"Well now—" assessing brown eyes were turned back on Ford "—we don't need a complaint to take an interest in the citizens of Scobey."

"I'm sure your citizens appreciate your diligence." Having grown up in a small town, Ford took the sheriff at his word. Which didn't mean he intended to tell the other man anything.

"What's your business in town?"

"That's between me and Ms. Adams."

"I've heard there have been complaints about the babies crying."

Ford's tolerance for the questioning dried up. He opened the back door next to Cody. He gestured inside. "Look for yourself, they're fine. They're still adjusting to the loss of their parents. They have the right to a few tears."

"I suppose they do." The sheriff hiked his pant legs and crouched to look in at the babies. Satisfied he rose to his standard six one. "Why are you sitting out here?"

Ford frowned to see Cody starting to stir. He quietly closed the door. "They aren't sleeping well, we took a drive to settle them down."

"Right. I'll let you go." Mitchell sounded disappointed he had no reason to detain Ford, and his next words held a clear warning. "Just take heed, Rachel Adams isn't alone here in Scobey."

"It's been snowing here for about an hour." Rachel frowned at the view outside the window. Dark clouds obscured the sun. Snow fell, pushed around by whistling gusts of wind. This weather had better not keep Sullivan from bringing back the twins. Maybe she should call him and tell him to come now.

"I can stop by on my way home." Sam Mitchell offered. "Make sure you're all right." He'd called to warn her an unexpected cold front was moving in fast and heavy.

Uh-huh.

He'd already mentioned running into Ford Sullivan in town. She bet. He'd probably hunted Sullivan down at his hotel.

"Mitch, I'm fine. There's no need to waste a trip out here."

She'd broken things off between them nearly two years ago, but the sheriff continued to take an interest in her affairs. Or lack of them, in the hope of reigniting the ardor between them. For an intelligent man, no one buried his head in the sand better than Mitch.

"I heard they're really missing you over at the clinic."

"Hmm."

"Mrs. Regent's Poopsy nipped a couple of the techs during her clipping."

"Rough."

"Yeah. Poopsy doesn't care for anyone but you. Rumor is Mrs. Regent won't be scheduling Poopsy again until you're back from maternity leave."

"Oh joy."

Rachel opened up a new e-mail, wondering, not for the first time, at the man's ability to basically hold a conversation on his own.

Only half listening, she sent her latest article off as an attachment, then closed down her computer. When she looked up, she spotted her SUV pull past the window.

Her glance immediately went to the clock. Sullivan was early. By almost three hours.

Yes!

"Mitch, I've got to go. Sullivan just pulled up with the babies."

"I still don't like the idea of you dealing with him on your own. You call me if you have any problems."

"He's a SEAL, Mitch. I'm either in great hands, or you'll never find the body."

"That's not funny."

"You're telling me." Not that she feared for her life. No, she feared for her peace of mind. Not only because he'd threatened to take the twins from her, but because she'd dreamed of exactly how great those hands would feel against her skin. Her blood heated with the memory of gentle caresses and not so soft strokes. Oh my.

A knock sounded at the door.

"Mitch, I'll be fine. Gotta go." She disconnected and headed for the door fanning herself en route. No way she wanted Sullivan to know he got her hot and bothered.

She opened the door and leaned against the threshold. Sullivan stood alone on the porch. "Sullivan. You're early."

He ran a hand through already mussed hair. The gesture was the first sign of vulnerability he'd displayed. Behind him snow fell from a gray sky—heavier now than a few minutes ago. White clusters covered wide shoulders and dark hair. It did her heart good to see him disheveled.

Red rose high on his cheeks. Rachel blinked, surprised by the sign of discomfort. But was it temper or embarrassment that lit up his features?

"Call me Ford, or Mustang if you prefer. Let me just get this out right up-front." He met her gaze straight on. "I'm sorry. I made assumptions I shouldn't have. You've done a phenomenal job handling Cody and Jolie alone over the past week. Thank you for being there for them."

Oh, unfair. Here she'd hoped for a moment of weakness and instead he showed his strength with a sincere apology. And he wanted her to call him Mustang? The picture of the beautiful range horses came to mind. Proud and wild, free and reckless, she had no problem seeing how he'd earned the nickname that played off his given name.

No, she'd stick with "Sullivan," much less intimate, more distancing.

"Enough already. In another minute you'll have me weeping." She pushed past him. "Let's get the babies inside out of the snow."

She dashed to the nearest door, freed Jolie from her seat and quickly returned to the house. Teeth chattering, because she hadn't bothered with a jacket, she arrowed straight for the fire.

She spread a blanket in the middle of the floor and set Jolie in the center with a couple of Matchbox cars. Then Rachel stepped back and watched Sullivan lower Cody to the blanket.

Moving away, she curled into the corner of the sofa while Sullivan stood taking in the room.

Nothing to be embarrassed about this time. She'd been busy for the last twenty-one hours. Well, okay, she'd slept for the first part of that time, but the rest had gone toward housework and laundry. Plus she'd gotten a couple of articles written for her syndicated column on animal manners.

"Place looks great."

"You don't." Jolie soon gave up on the toy cars to crawl across the living room carpet straight for Rachel. She lifted the girl into her lap. "How much sleep did you get last night?"

"I've had less." He shrugged away her concern. "It's not the lack of sleep that got to me. It's the helplessness. I'm a man of action, but nothing I did was right."

"That's how it was for me for the first three days, then they finally began to calm down." Okay, this conversation wasn't so bad.

He even made her laugh when he told her how he'd found the cereal in the bottom of the baby bag, but since he didn't have high chairs he'd taken the twins out to their car seats and fed them in the SUV. Smart actually, but she'd had no doubt of his intelligence since the moment she'd first opened the door to him.

"At least they stopped crying long enough to eat." Sullivan bent to pick up Cody who was trying to climb his leg.

"They take comfort from each other." Rachel ran her fingers through Jolie's soft hair.

The look he sent her spoke volumes. "You mean they feed off each other's emotions. One starts crying, and they try to outdo each other."

"You have to remember they're traumatized." She defended her niece and nephew. "They've lost their parents. That's going to take time to get over."

"Yeah." The fire popped and shifted. Sullivan walked over to tend it, easily handling both Cody and the fire poker. "The sooner they're settled the better. Have you considered signing the papers?"

Disappointment washed through Rachel. Back to square one. But she wouldn't be signing any papers. Now or later.

"I'm thinking you should be the one signing the papers," she challenged.

Before he could respond, the lights flickered. Once. Twice. Then they settled.

"Shoot." Holding Jolie close, Rachel leaped to her feet and headed for the front window. A wall of white fell heavily. Actually it blew sideways, the wind's force strong enough to blow the snow horizontal, confirming her worst fears.

The storm had become a blizzard.

"Looks bad." Sullivan stood behind her.

She smelled the clean scent of him. Musk, starch and man, an intoxicating mix. Almost distracting enough to take her attention from the storm.

But that would be a deadly mistake.

"Yeah. Blizzard. Damn, there was no mention of snow in the weather reports earlier." Obviously she should have paid better attention to Mitch.

"Won't be the first time they've been wrong."

The understated response startled a laugh from Rachel. "You've got that right."

Already her SUV was buried under several inches of snow and ice. It needed to be moved to the garage or the engine would freeze.

The lights flickered again. And again they came back steady.

That wouldn't last.

"Do you have a generator?" he asked.

She nodded. "Fuel is in the barn."

Lord, she hoped she had enough fuel to weather the storm. Living alone, she'd learned to be prepared, but a lightning storm in late September had hit a power tower east of Scobey, knocking her power out. She hadn't had a chance to restock before receiving the news about Crystal. Since then she'd been so busy with the twins, she hadn't thought about restocking her emergency supplies.

"I should leave. The hotel will probably let me back in without the twins."

"You can't drive in this." She handed Jolie to Sullivan and then moved to the closet to yank out her jacket and some boots. "Give me my keys."

"I've driven in worse."

"So you're looking to leave me alone with the babies again?" One boot on, one boot off, she propped her hands on her hips. "Look, I don't want you here any more than you want to stay, but I wouldn't send my worst enemy out in a storm this bad. Oh wait, you are my worst enemy."

He lifted a brow as he rocked the babies, but he only said, "We're only six miles from town."

"Only?" She stomped into her other boot. God save her from ignorant tourists. "Where are you from?"

"Southern California. But I've trained in all forms of extreme weather."

"I've no doubt. But there's no need to go all SEAL on me. Now, hand over the keys."

Sullivan frowned his displeasure as he glanced out of the window. "You can't go out there, either."

"I have to. If the SUV isn't moved, the cold will crack the engine block."

"I'll move it."

She shook her head as she wrapped a scarf around her throat and ears. "I need to get fuel for the generator, too. And bring in some wood."

He stepped into her path. "I can do it."

"Look, you're helping by being here to watch the twins." She pulled on her gloves, waiting for him to step aside. "I know what I'm doing."

Giving in, he juggled the babies to reach the keys in his pants pocket, which he handed to her. "Be careful."

"Always. Candles and matches are in the kitchen cupboard to the left of the sink. In case the lights go out before I get back with fuel for the generator."

Ducking into the closet again, she looped a heavy coil of rope over her shoulder.

"What's that for?" Sullivan demanded.

"Snow line. One end hooks to the front porch post, the other I hook around my waist. It acts as an anchor so I can find my way back to the house."

A grim look settled over his features. "This is ridiculous. I can't let you go out there alone."

"Didn't we just have this conversation? I live alone, Sullivan. I do what I need to survive. That doesn't change just because your macho self is here." She pulled a second pair of gloves from her coat pocket and donned them over the first pair. "And I don't have time to argue."

Not waiting for a response, she moved to the door, stepped out and quickly pulled it closed behind her.

Ford looked down at the babies in his arms. Their care and safety had to be a priority, but it didn't feel right letting Rachel struggle against the elements on her own.

He carried the twins to the playpen. Both babies immediately crawled to the side and pulled themselves up. He tossed a few of the plastic blocks in to keep them occupied. Neither Cody nor Jolie paid any attention to the blocks.

"Ba da da sa." Cody registered his complaint and lifted his arms to be picked up.

"Maa ga do." Jolie put her two cents in and held her arms up, too.

He itched to go to the window and check on Rachel's progress but moved to the fireplace instead. The fire had died down to mere embers. He tossed on a new log, then began to pace, wearing a path in the dove-gray carpet.

"What do you say, Cody, we're the men here. It's up to us to protect the women. And that's not happening with us in here and her out there."

"Mamama?" Jolie stuck her finger in her mouth.

Ford stopped midstride and stared at Jolie. How odd to hear her call Rachel mama or almost mama, he reasoned. But still, it sounded wrong. Felt wrong. And brought home to him how much life had changed in such a short period of time.

Tony and Crystal were gone, killed in an earthquake while visiting a Mexican resort.

Ford had been shocked to return from assignment to learn he was guardian of Tony's children. Yeah, he'd agreed to take on the responsibility, but he'd never really expected it to be necessary. Certainly not so soon. But prepared or not, Ford owed Tony. He'd saved Ford's life; honor and friendship demanded Ford step up to meet Tony's last request.

Tony had always envied Ford his close family, so much so that he'd arranged for Ford to raise his kids. Which meant the twins went home with Ford. He'd be moving in with Gram, who had agreed to watch the babies for him. He'd also be hiring a full-time nanny.

Ford didn't want to hurt Rachel, but it couldn't be helped.

The storm, however, managed to delay the inevitable.

Rachel really surprised him. Her aquamarine eyes and white-gold hair cut short and sassy hid a depth of passion he'd bet few people saw.

Frustrating as her protectiveness was, he respected her spirit, her willingness to put herself on the line for the children in her care.

He just needed to convince her they'd be better off with him.

After he saved her from the freezing hell outside.

For all her feistiness and lean strength, she had to weigh next to nothing. She'd whip around on the end of that snow line like a kite in a hurricane.

It'd only been five minutes, but he couldn't take this. Gram had taught him better than to sit on his butt while a woman did the hard chores. Forget endangering herself in a storm of this caliber.

Checking on the babies, he found the sleepless night had caught up with them. Curled together they slept peacefully.

"Now that's what I call team players." He tossed a blanket over them. "You hang tight. I'm going to help Rachel."

Cold attacked Rachel from all sides, freezing exposed skin, slowing her down, making each breath cut like ice. Snow and hail pelted the windshield, making it hard to see.

The engine refused to turn over the first few tries. She worried it may be too late to move. Crossing her fingers, she gave it one more try and breathed easier when the engine fired up.

Thank God. She didn't want Sullivan stuck here any longer than necessary. Unfortunately necessary looked like several days at the moment. Just damn.

And to top it off, when the weather cleared Sullivan expected her to hand the twins over to him, never to be seen again. She couldn't even think about that without choking up.

So she wouldn't think about it.

As if.

While she waited for the engine to warm, Rachel rested her head against the steering wheel and worried about what she was going to do if Sullivan fought for custody of the twins.

She lived in a one-bedroom house in Scobey, Montana, population barely topping a thousand. And she worked as a veterinarian technician at a pet clinic because she liked dealing with animals better than dealing with people.

Wind buffeted the car as she worried about what she had to offer the twins besides cramped quarters and nonexistent social skills.

A home. A warm touch in the middle of the night. Someone in the world to belong to. The answers came from deep in her soul where she kept her secret hopes and dreams hidden from the light of day.

Belonging. It was no small thing. Rachel vowed she'd fight to give Cody and Jolie a sense of belonging.

Because damn, she never thought she could love this deeply or this quickly.

And no one, not Sullivan, not anyone, was going to take them from her.

Lifting her head, she reached for the gearshift.

Next to her the door suddenly opened. She jumped and screamed.

CHAPTER THREE

SULLIVAN stood framed in the opening of the SUV door.

"Jerk," Rachel shouted. "You scared me. What are you doing out here?"

"I came...help."

The storm stole part of his reply, but she got the gist. She yelled out her own concern. "Babies?"

He leaned down so he spoke directly into her ear. "Playpen. Sleeping. Scoot over so we can get this done and get back inside."

She shook her head. No way was she climbing over the gearshift in the bulky jacket and boots. "Go around."

Surprisingly he did so without argument.

Rachel drove the thirty feet to the old-barn-turned-garage at a crawl. She left the SUV idling while Sullivan braved the storm to open the big barn doors. Inside, she found an old blanket and they covered the vehicle.

"I could have handled this on my own." She advised him resentfully as she tugged on her end of the blanket.

"Pull in your claws, wildcat. This has nothing to do with your abilities." He didn't look up from anchoring his end. "I was raised better than to let you do it on your own."

Damn him for making her sound hysterical. "The babies aren't safe alone inside."

"All the more reason to work together so we can get back to them quickly." He came around from the front of the SUV. He wore her yellow raincoat, which dwarfed her but fit him just right.

He looked strong, calm, confident and a little amused as he grabbed his duffel bag from the back seat.

She moved away from him to where she stored the generator fuel. Her heart sank when she saw she only had enough fuel for a couple of days.

Sullivan crowded close to reach the fuel. "Is this it?"

Rachel bristled. "I don't usually let it get so low. I've been a little distracted since the twins came to live with me."

Her whole world had shifted with the arrival of Cody and Jolie. Luckily the pet clinic had given her maternity leave because she'd been so busy getting them settled, becoming accustomed to their presence and schedule, everything else, including her writing had suffered.

She hadn't taken proper care with her normal chores, which in this case could prove costly.

"Cut yourself some slack. You've had a big adjustment to make." He shook a can. "How long will this last?"

His simple understanding floored her. And deflated her snit.

"A couple of days, more if we're careful. We'll probably loose electricity, but we have plenty of wood and propane. And a well-stocked freezer."

If she had any luck at all, the blizzard would be over before they ran out of fuel.

Of course it would take another day or two for the roads to be cleared after the snow stopped. Extra time with a man hot enough to give Brad Pitt a run for his money and who had an unsettling habit of reacting in the way she least expected. And two babies still fretful after suffering the biggest tragedy of their young lives.

Oh joy.

"So we'll be careful," he said with a confidence that indicated he was used to handling difficult situations. "Do we need anything else from here?"

"Yeah." She opened a cupboard and took down a large flashlight. "This is it."

He took the flashlight from her and led the way outside. She stood shivering while he closed the barn doors.

Turning toward the house, she encountered a moving wall of white.

Teeth chattering, hands shaking, she pulled on the snow line until it grew taut, a chore made more difficult because she could no longer feel her fingers.

Sullivan's hand joined hers on the rope. He surrounded her with his strength and warmth, urging her forward. She started for the house.

The last of the light had gone so Sullivan used the flashlight; even so, she saw little beyond her own hands on the rope.

It was hard going, the exertion exhausting, the cold debilitating. Every step became a battle of will against nature. The protection of his bulk sheltered her from the worst of the storm and helped move them along. By the time she spotted the corner of the porch she was truly grateful for Sullivan's help.

The lights were out. She worried about the babies alone inside. Hopefully enough light would come from the fire that they wouldn't get too frightened.

She stopped and indicated the shed on the side of the house. "We need to fill the wood reservoir," she shouted. "We may not be able to get outside for days."

He spoke next to her ear. "I'll do it. You need to get out of this weather."

"I…help."

"Save the heroics. Your teeth are about to crack from the chattering."

He helped her the rest of the way to the porch and handed her the gasoline and flashlight. She leaned close to instruct him on the location of the reservoir door on the outside of the house.

He nodded his comprehension. "Get inside. Take care of the babies." He turned away.

She caught his arm, stopping him. "The rope." She found the hook at her waist and tried to release it.

"Don't need it. I'll be close to the house."

He started to leave again. But fear clutched her gut and she grabbed his coat. "No. Take the rope."

Rather than argue further, he threaded the rope through the layers of his clothes and clicked the hook to his belt.

Once he was rigged up, he stepped over to her rather than away. He tucked her scarf up around her ears. "Get inside where it's warm. I'll be back."

Half frozen, exhausted, and more worried about him than she cared to admit, Rachel let herself inside the house dragging the fuel and lanterns in with her.

She couldn't stop shivering. Even the marrow in her bones felt frozen.

Below the icy discomfort and the natural concern of being cut off from the rest of the world, she was just plain pissed at the quirk of fate that made her anxious for the safety of the man responsible for tearing her life apart.

But then why should life suddenly start playing fair?

After stripping off her soggy outdoor gear, Rachel breathed on her hands to warm them as she stumbled to the laundry room just off the kitchen. She kept a flashlight and candle on a shelf inside the door. She quickly got the generator going and then went to check on the babies.

Her heart melted when she found them cuddled together sleeping. She swayed in relief. Clutching the cushioned rail, she held on tight. She stood lost in awe at the sheer innocence and resourcefulness of them.

After a while she heard the door, felt an icy draft of air.

"How are they doing?" Sullivan appeared next to her.

Emotions more mixed than ever, she moved her gaze to him, noted his damp hair and skin still flushed from the cold. She'd never admit it to him, but she'd been really glad to see him out there.

"Fine. They're still sleeping."

"They look so peaceful."

"Yeah," she turned away to hide the tears in her eyes. "Too bad it won't last."

"What's that supposed to mean?"

Temper spun her back around. "I mean if you have your way, the little bit of normalcy they've found since losing their parents will be torn away from them by the very people they should be able to trust."

He scowled. "It's not like that."

"It's exactly like that, but you can forget it. I'm not giving them up."

"Hey, hey." He framed her face, caught an escaped tear on his thumb. "I know this is hard. But my friend and your sister entrusted their children to our care because they knew we'd do right by them. Even when it's hard."

The fight went out of her.

"It's not fair." She pulled away from his touch, from the pity in his eyes.

He easily stalled her attempt to distance herself and folded her into his arms instead.

"No." He agreed. "It's not. But you're not alone. We'll help each other through this."

She wanted to riot against him, to push him away and deny his reasonableness. But it felt too good to lean on someone for a change. Someone with a hard chest and muscular arms, who smelled like a dream and warmed her with the heat of his body. Giving in, she laid her head on his shoulder and closed her eyes so he couldn't see her anguish.

"I don't want to like you."

His chest rumbled under her ear when he laughed, and he stroked her hair like she stroked Cody when she held him. The tender caress both soothed and unnerved.

"Well hold onto that thought, tomorrow is another day. Listen, you're cold, tired and hungry. We'll postpone talk of custody for now. Why don't you go take a shower while I fix some dinner."

The truce, like the shower, sounded like heaven. "We should probably conserve the hot water."

"Not tonight. We need to thaw out. You go first while I check out the kitchen."

"The twins?"

His chest lifted and fell on a heavy sigh. "Let them sleep. They didn't get much rest last night."

"They haven't slept well over the last week." Which, except for last night, equated to the same for her. Maybe that's why she felt like she could sleep just like this, standing up with her head on his shoulder listening to the steady beat of his heart. "They've been through so much."

He gave her a squeeze. "It'll get better with time."

He gave out heat like a furnace, thawing not only the chill from her bones but also the frigid wall around her heart. How long had it been since she'd been comforted by a man like this?

Never. Certainly not by the man she'd called father.

The thought was enough to have her pulling away and backing up. She had no business leaning on any man, least of all this man. So he had a point with his argument that the babies' parents had trusted them to do right by their children. That didn't mean she could trust *him*.

His opinion and hers hadn't gelled yet when it came to the twins.

She debated whether to leave him alone with them but there was little enough he could do. The storm prevented him leaving and he'd proven his gentleness when dealing with them.

"I'll go take that shower." She turned toward the one

bedroom. When she reached the door, she glanced back. "Thank you."

He'd been watching her, more accurately he'd been watching her butt. He raised his gaze to meet her eyes; no apology there for being caught enjoying the view, just simple male appreciation. He lifted his chin in a gesture of acknowledgment.

A small thrill warmed her, raising every feminine instinct she kept ruthlessly suppressed.

She closed the door between them, deliberately placing a barrier between her and the dangerous man who awakened feelings she preferred to keep buried.

Time to get a grip. How could she spend even a moment in her enemy's arms? No exaggeration. Anyone wanting to take the twins from her rated as an enemy.

Really she didn't understand why he wanted the twins. As a SEAL and bachelor—his commanding officer had also shared that bit of information—taking on the twins could only be a hardship, even with family to help.

Or maybe he meant for his family to absorb the burden.

Family. Definitely her weak point.

In the bathroom she stripped down and stepped into the shower letting the cascade of hot water soak the cold away.

Her thoughts turned to Crystal. When Rachel had left home, her biggest regret in walking away was in leaving ten year old Crystal behind. But Rachel couldn't stay where she wasn't wanted.

On her seventeenth birthday, she'd learned that the man she'd always known as her dad wasn't her biological father. The news had devastated her, yet explained so much. Like why she'd always felt like an outsider in her own home.

Beginning to thaw out now, she reached for her favorite peach scented soap.

Dan had gotten a raw deal. Rachel had understood that. He'd been lied to, tricked into raising another man's child. Yet he'd fed and clothed her, never beat her. Plenty of other kids had had it worse.

Rachel blamed her mother. She was the one who had lied, who had traded one man's child for another man's pride. Who had traded her child's comfort for her own. Stella Adams could have given Rachel the things Dan denied her: time, attention, affection. But Stella chose not to rock the boat.

For that Rachel had never forgiven her.

After rinsing, she turned off the water and stepped out of the tub. Wrapped in a large towel, she moved into the bedroom.

Rachel had learned her lesson too well in childhood to easily change now. Rather than chance heartache, she preferred her own company. Sure, she'd had relationships, but they never really went anywhere. Her fault. She wasn't willing to put her heart on the line and risk being rejected by someone she loved.

Not again.

Unfortunately her relationship with her sister had been a casualty of that lesson. But contrary to Sullivan's allegations, they'd forged a new kinship after their parents' death.

Rachel refused to believe Crystal had been faking the rapport they'd shared.

Dressed in thick socks and old sweats, she entered the living room, stopping to check on the still sleeping babies before moving on to the kitchen. She'd expected Sullivan to open a couple of cans of soup, but she'd underestimated him. The scent of garlic and tomatoes made her stomach grumble.

"Smells good."

He looked up from where he was buttering bread. "It is," he said with confidence. "Spaghetti. I thought we needed something hardy."

He'd changed out of his wet clothes while she'd been in the tub. The jeans and gray T-shirt displayed his masculinity to advantage. The casual clothes should have minimized his appearance, instead they emphasized his broad shoulders, muscular thighs, firm butt.

A dark lock of hair fell forward on his forehead. She fought an uncharacteristic desire to sweep it back, to feel the tactile softness against her fingers.

Remembering too well how it had felt to be in his arms, she moved to the refrigerator and pulled out a head of lettuce. She needed something to keep her hands, and her thoughts, busy.

"Why don't you grab your shower while the bread toasts?" She urged him. While she'd been dressing, she'd come to a decision. The less time she spent in his company the better. Not an easy chore considering they were stuck together in a one-bedroom house, but she was committed to the act of self-preservation. "I'll make a salad."

He washed and dried his hands. "Sounds like a plan."

Opening the preheated oven, he bent to insert the garlic bread.

Rachel's hormones, usually under strict control, chose now to go astray. She wanted nothing more than to walk over, plunge her hands in his back pockets and squeeze.

Luckily he straightened before she gave in to the impulse.

She cleared her throat. "I put a towel out for you."

"Thanks." He grabbed his duffel bag and disappeared into the bathroom.

She breathed a sigh of relief. He took up so much space in a room. His very presence energized the air. Her recent trip down memory lane served to remind her exactly why she needed to keep him at arm's length. She had everything to lose and nothing to gain.

He came from a different world, here only as long as it would take to shatter her life.

A whimper drew her to the playpen in the living room. Jolie stirred. Rachel tucked a blanket around the little girl and then gently patted her back until she settled down to sleep. Cody didn't stir.

Would they be better off with Sullivan? He'd mentioned a large family, supportive and close-knit. Everything she'd dreamed of as a child.

Yet it seemed a betrayal to the children she'd come to love to even think the question.

Hearing the water go off in the shower spurred her to action. She caught the bread while it was still golden-brown. The salad went together quickly with a course chopping of lettuce and chives and quartered tomatoes.

By the time Sullivan came out of the bathroom, once again dressed in jeans and T-shirt, she had the table set. "Dinner is ready."

"Great." Ford slicked his fingers through damp hair before moving to hold Rachel's chair out for her.

She frowned at the gesture, suspicion alive in those amazing aquamarine eyes. "Who are you trying to impress?" She demanded. "We're not on a date."

Now why did he find her prickliness so appealing? "Blame my upbringing. Gram believes in old-fashioned courtesies."

"Thank you." The words were grudging as she slid into her chair. "You were raised by your grandmother?"

He nodded as he claimed his own seat. "Since I was eight."

"Hmm."

"She raised my five brothers and me after my parents died in an automobile accident."

Her eyes flashed to his then away. "I'm sorry."

Okay, less grudging but still a conversational dead end. He got the feeling she was good at dodging discussion.

Watching the tines of her fork slide through plum-pink lips, Ford fought off the sensual memory of how sweet she'd felt in his arms. Another time and place and he'd be making major moves on her. But he was already guaranteed to bring heartbreak before he left. No sense complicating the situation by acting on the attraction he felt for her.

Which didn't mean he'd allow her to ignore him.

He sent her a chiding glance. "Let me know if I'm boring you."

The cutest thing happened. Her earlobes turned red! And though agitation came and went in her sea-foam eyes, she made an effort to participate in the conversation.

"That must have been a difficult childhood."

"It was tough losing my parents, but Gram loved us and we were able to stay together. That counted for a lot." He leaned forward on his elbows. "You're not very talkative, are you?"

She swallowed a bite of spaghetti. "No."

"Why not?" He speared a tomato.

Silence greeted his question. She obviously didn't want to respond but he waited her out.

With a sigh she finally answered. "Generally because I prefer my own company."

"And in this case?"

"I don't know much about this topic." As if that revealed too much, she added, "And I see no need for us to become all buddy-buddy."

He ignored the dismissal. "What did you mean when you said you'd failed your sister?"

Her eyes flashed. "I'm not talking to you about my sister. You're wrong about her."

What a fake she was. For all her cold facade, she was all heat and passion underneath. And so incredibly vulnerable. Whatever happened in her family, it had left her hurting.

"Crystal said you ran away from home. Why? Family is important."

"Yeah. And I'm all the family the twins have."

Stubborn woman. Yet her relentlessness demonstrated her protective feelings toward the babies. Much as he wanted to exploit her weaknesses, Ford couldn't fault her for that.

"Tell me why you left home," he said.

She cocked her head causing a white-blond lock of hair to fall into her eyes. A quick flick of her hand sent it back into place.

"I know what you're doing, you know."

He hesitated for a heartbeat. "And what is that?"

"Information is power." Rachel drew circles on the table with the condensation from her ice water; a small frown drew her light brown brows together in concentration. "You want me to tell you about my past so you can use it against me to get what you want."

She was right. "I shared my history with you."

"For a purpose." She slanted him a wry glance. "No doubt I'm supposed to believe the twins would benefit from all the male influence tempered by the sweet little grandmother."

"Maybe I'm just making conversation."

She cocked an eyebrow. "Please. All is fair in love and war. And you're a warrior to the bone."

"Very clever." He raised his glass of water in acknowledgment.

"Now why do I feel that surprises you?"

Unabashed, he grinned. "Everything about you surprises me."

"Gee thanks." She clinked her glass against his then sipped. "Considering you think of me as a lazy deadbeat who can't maintain a relationship, I'll take that as a compliment."

He laughed, enjoying the note of humor mixed with the censure.

"I admit I had a few misconceptions. Your courage,

patience and dedication were totally unexpected. In my job we put emotion aside to complete the task."

Now *he'd* revealed too much, which hadn't been part of his plan at all. Her quick wit and intelligent eyes made talking to her too easy. And too dangerous. Avoiding her speculative gaze, he stood and carried his dishes to the sink.

She looked as if she wanted to pursue the topic, but thankfully her habitual reticence kicked in.

"I'm beat." Feeling he'd dodged a bullet, he pushed away from the counter. "What do you say we get these dishes done and go to bed?"

CHAPTER FOUR

Go to bed. Go to bed. Go to bed. The words echoed and bounced around the room, bringing to mind images of bare skin, tangled limbs, clinging mouths.

Unnerving to say the least. More so because Rachel was less disturbed imagining him naked than she had any right to be.

Her nipples tightened and her loins clenched around an emptiness she longed to assuage.

Embarrassed by her reaction, because of course he didn't mean they should sleep *together,* she avoided his gaze by clearing the table. Even so, she felt the heat rise in her cheeks, staining them red. Her ire rose, too, because only part of the heightened color came from mortification.

The rest was desire, pure and sinful.

Just because she preferred her own company these days didn't mean she didn't know what to do with a man when she got him in her clutches.

As she neared the counter, she noticed the clock on the oven: 7:03.

"It's only seven o'clock." She pointed out. So much

had happened in the last few hours it seemed much later. "A little early for bed."

He checked his watch, then grinned wryly. "Is that all? Must be feeling the effects of yesterday's early start. And did I mention the twins didn't get much sleep last night?"

"You did." She started the water running in the sink, splashed in some soap. She supposed she owed him for her best sleep in days. "Why don't you—"

"Oh." She jumped when she turned and came face-to-face with Sullivan. Instinctively stepping back, she slipped in some water on the floor and she felt herself going down.

"Careful." Lightning fast Sullivan caught her against his hard length. "I've got you."

Startled to find herself in his arms again, she looked up and found only inches separated her from blue eyes filled with stark longing.

She blinked and met a gaze devoid of all emotion.

That fast. Which begged the question if he'd felt anything at all. Or if she'd projected her own longing onto him.

"Sorry," she said, quickly pushing away. He let her go, a little too easily for her ego. Chiding herself for the foolish pang, she hiked up her sleeves and plunged her hands into the sudsy water.

"Did you drive all the way here, or fly?" She latched onto his comment about his trip, determined to maintain a conversation to dispel the awkwardness.

"I drove." Dishcloth in hand, he started drying.

She watched him out of the corner of her eye as they made quick work of the dishes. In her experience men avoided household chores. Likely she had Sullivan's grandmother to thank for his thoughtfulness.

Rachel appreciated his help, if not his proximity.

"Easier that way to pack them into your Jeep and take them home with you." She had no illusions about his strategy.

He lifted one shoulder, let it fall. "That's the plan."

Present tense. So he hadn't changed his mind about the twins even though his impressions of her had improved. Disheartened, she fell silent.

A whimper from the direction of the living room disrupted the moment. The babies were stirring.

"I'll go." Sullivan moved past her into the living room, headed toward the playpen.

Reminded why she kept her own company, she picked up the dishcloth, folded it over the drawer handle and slowly followed.

"Hey, Cody." He lifted the boy into his arms. "How're you doing? Are you hungry? It's time for dinner."

Cody stopped crying and laid his head on Sullivan's shoulder.

Jolie held her arms up for Rachel to lift her, too. Rachel swooped the girl into a big hug. And discovered a desperate need for a diaper change.

The next hour and a half was spent taking care of that problem, feeding the babies and getting them ready for bed.

"There's only the one bedroom. Which is where the crib is." Rachel gave Sullivan the layout. She indicated the slate-blue, ultra-suede sofa. "You can take the couch. I'll get you some blankets."

"This will be fine." He eyed the overstuffed cushions dubiously. With good reason, considering the length fell short of his six-two frame by six inches.

Leaving him to the logistics, she gathered the extra bedding from the hall closet.

Back in the living room, the babies played in the playpen, and Sullivan had the wood closet open as he restocked the oversized basket near the fireplace. A nice blaze burned in the old grate.

The lights in the kitchen had been extinguished, and he'd lit the candles on the credenza behind the couch giving the room a cozy feel.

The whole scene smacked of domestic tranquility. Way too home and hearth for her. It struck her as wrong. Because it felt too right. Sullivan was a stranger, an interloper. They shouldn't be so comfortable with each other, so easy together.

Time for a tactical retreat.

"Here you go." She dropped the bedding on the end of the couch. He was a big boy; he could make his own bed. "I'm beat. And it's past the babies' bedtime. We're for bed."

He closed the door to the wood closet and dusted off his hands. "Thanks. Do you think the storm will be gone by morning?"

"Hard to tell." Did his question mean he felt as antsy as she did? "We weren't expecting snow, but it was supposed to rain for several days."

"How long before the roads get cleared after a storm like this?"

"Why? You suddenly need to be somewhere?"

"Other than getting the twins home and settled? No."

He ran a weary hand through his dark hair. "I was thinking of the fuel levels."

"Right. We need to shut down the generator. That's what we're short on. The heat is on propane, so we're okay there."

"And we have plenty of wood."

Amused, she propped her hands on her hips. "Listen to Mr. California"

He crossed to the couch and started putting his bed together. "We do get snow in California you know." With a flex of biceps the size of ham hocks, he tossed the pillows into the corner. "Paradise Pines is in the mountains east of San Diego. We usually get snow once or twice a year."

Carefully keeping her distance from Sullivan, because she was inordinately tempted to test the strength of those biceps, it took Rachel a minute to process what he'd said.

She blamed her distraction on him. Unused to having strangers in her home, especially tall, muscular he-men intent on taking her cherished wards from her, her normal instincts were off.

She laughed. "And it lasts for what, a day and a half? Please. We lose the refrigerator with the generator. I'll bag up some snow to put inside to keep things cold."

"Okay." He nodded toward the kitchen. "You take care of the snow, I'll get the generator."

Surprised and pleased by his easy acceptance of her opinion, she grabbed a flashlight and headed for the drawer with the extra large plastic bags.

Oh, yeah, he was a mystery. As was the way he made her feel.

Not willing to explore the thought, she made quick

work of filling several bags with snow from the back stoop and placing them strategically throughout the refrigerator.

Back in the living room she watched him move his duffel bag from the end of the couch to the head of the couch, then toe off his shoes and place them next to the duffel. He nodded toward the playpen. "Those two are out for the count."

Rachel checked on the twins. Cody and Jolie were once again sleeping curled up together. They looked so peaceful.

"Darn. I hate to disturb them. I know from experience if I wake them just to put them to bed, they'll fight sleep like heavy-weight contenders fight for the belt."

"So let them sleep. I'll be right here if they wake up."

"I'm not sure that's a good idea." No, giving control to this man was definitely not a good idea. What if he took the twins in the middle of the night?

What, her more rational side scoffed, and hike six miles to town in a blizzard?

Not so strange, the mother in her argued, he was a SEAL after all.

Sensing her turmoil, he met her gaze straight-on and held up his right hand as if making a vow. "I promise, they're safe with me. Come on, Rachel, we all need a good night's sleep."

"All right, but I'll leave my door open to listen for them."

"I'm not going to make off with them, Rachel."

"Excuse me if I'm wary. I just met you." God, was it only yesterday? "What you say and what you do could be two different things."

"No, I'm a man of honor. My C.O. told you so, remember?" His expression said he didn't like being doubted. As a SEAL, she'd think he'd be used to questioning actions and motives and having them questioned in turn.

Was it her? Did he care what she thought of him?

A tingle ran down her spine.

"Oh, yeah. Man of honor. I forgot." She turned her back on the titillating sensation and on him.

At her bedroom door she halted to face him but forgot what she meant to say as the words suffocated for lack of breath.

Sullivan stood folding his T-shirt, firelight danced on his naked skin, his sleek muscles. Boy was he ripped. Dark hair lightly covered his chest narrowing over his six-pack to low riding jeans.

When his hands moved to his zipper, she gasped, inhaling much needed air.

"Good night." Executing an abrupt about-face, she dodged into her room, one thought clear in her mind. She was in serious danger of falling in lust.

Rachel woke to a gloomy room and the smell of coffee. Under the circumstances, she'd feared she wouldn't be able to sleep, but the last thing she remembered was planning to work on her book à la Abe Lincoln style.

A couple of months ago a publisher, enamored with her syndicated animal antics column, approached her asking for a book on animal manners. She'd been intrigued enough to send out a proposal.

That was before she got the call regarding the children.

Catching sight of the time, eight-thirty, she bounded out of bed. She never slept this late. The babies never slept this late.

Spiking fingers through her tousled hair, she padded in her sweats and socks into the living room. And found the babies where she'd left them last night, sleeping in the playpen. A change of clothes proved they'd been up and about at some point.

Ford was doing double duty. Trying to soften her up by letting her sleep in again. Darn him for being considerate. It wouldn't change her mind.

A rush of love swelled her heart. She bent and ran her hand over Jolie's silky brown hair. More than anything she wanted to do right by Jolie and Cody. She prayed that wouldn't mean giving them up.

Before straightening she traced a finger over Cody's rosy cheek. Whatever happened, the twins were innocents.

A bang in the kitchen spun her in that direction.

Ford stood, arms braced on the granite counter, head hanging between those amazing biceps. Silhouetted by the window, the violence of the storm outside embodied his internal struggle.

Obviously a private moment.

Rachel back pedaled to give him his privacy. Until he reared back and slammed his fist into the granite, bloodying his knuckles.

Shocked, she stood rooted to the spot. The fierce action exposed a well of anger and grief. *Unresolved* anger and grief. She debated whether to go forward or leave him be.

He drew his arm back for another strike.

"Stop." Rachel lunged forward and grabbed onto his arm with both hands.

Not the smartest move she'd ever made.

Before she'd felt more than the flex of muscle, he'd hooked a foot around her ankle and taken her down to the floor. Blue eyes savage, his body blanketed hers, his forearm pressed hard against her windpipe.

Oh, yeah, he definitely had a dangerous edge.

By rights she should be terrified right about now. But fear wasn't the emotion sending shivers through her body.

He blinked then instantly relaxed his arm.

"Oh God." Unbelievably he lowered his forehead to rest on hers. "I'm sorry."

"Apology accepted." She lay completely still. "You can get off me now."

He didn't move. "I usually have more control."

She bet. "That's good to know."

"It's not smart to grab me."

"I'll remember that." Tentatively she moved her upper body, reminding him he still held her pinned. The movement rubbed her breasts against his chest. Her nipples responded to the contact.

So did his body.

She froze. And looked up into features drawn taut with desire. His gaze locked on her lips, and he began to lower his head.

A baby's cry broke the tension.

Reminded they weren't alone—how could she have forgotten his whole reason for being here? Rachel pushed Ford's shoulders until he rolled off her.

"Don't do that again." On her feet, she straightened her clothes and dusted her butt. And carefully avoided his eyes.

Sure, she felt the attraction between them, saw the want in his eyes. In another time or place, she might be willing to blow off some steam in a no-strings fling. But she had too much to lose with this man in this situation.

No matter how tempted she might be.

He forced her to look at him when he invaded her space. Towering over her, his gaze lingered on her mouth before rising to meet her eyes. "You have my word I won't attack you again."

She scowled at him. "That's not what I was referring to."

He crowded close to gently tuck a wild curl behind her ear. "It's the best you're going to get."

Ruthlessly squashing the thrill the warning gave her, she pushed past him to check on the babies. Not surprisingly they were awake and wanting to play. To keep them occupied while she dressed, she dumped a handful of toys into the playpen.

She escaped to her room to brush her teeth and change into jeans and a sweater. Mixed feelings kept her company. Such a luxury to go through her morning routine without feeling rushed or worried the twins would wake before she finished. Yet she felt bad for enjoying the indulgence because she loved Jolie and Cody, and they were totally dependent on her.

She both resented and appreciated Ford for giving her these moments of freedom. For allowing her a full night's sleep.

Back in the living room she spread a blanket on the

carpet in front of the fireplace and let the babies loose to crawl around. And when they started to wind down, she picked out several of their favorite books then tucked a baby on either side of her on the couch and spent the better part of the next hour reading to them.

Ford spent the time roaming the room. She tried not to think of his big, long-fingered hands touching her things. The sound of the drawer opening and closing in the credenza told her he'd found the broken bit. One side had pulled free of the front of the drawer. It looked like it should notch together but a set of staples prevented the pieces from connecting. She hadn't scraped together two minutes to fix it.

As she read on, he went to the utility closet next to where the generator ran, and retrieved her toolbox. She heard the clunk of it hitting the ground near the credenza behind her.

She finished the story then let the wiggling babies free. They immediately popped up to look over the back of the couch to see what Ford was doing. Rachel moved so she could keep track of the babies, ensuring neither fell backward or climbed over the top.

The new position gave her a premium view of one prime butt as Ford bent to look at the credenza from the bottom up.

Ford? Since when did she start thinking of the enemy by his first name? Maybe since he'd proved he wasn't the enemy by helping her in the snow, cooking her dinner and letting her sleep in.

All signs of a good guy.

Or a clever way to throw her off. Combined with his

penchant for touching her at every opportunity and the smoldering glances he constantly sent her way, the strategy was working.

She reminded herself of her plan to keep her distance from him.

"You don't have to do that," she told him.

Sitting back on his haunches, he shrugged, his attention fixed on the screwdriver he wielded. "It's no problem."

"You don't need to be doing things for me." She kept her tone cool. No need for him to know he was getting to her. "I can take care of my own children. Do my own chores."

"I like to keep busy." He eyed her over his shoulder. "It's not a crime to accept a little help sometimes."

"When you live alone, self-sufficiency is important."

"So is making friends of your neighbors."

"Baa da ha." Cody dug his toes into the cushion and pulled himself up.

"Oh?" She ringed Cody's ankle, pulled him gently down. "I've never found that to be the case."

"Ha da ca." Jolie bounced up and down.

Ford's gaze challenged Rachel. "Have you ever tried?"

She stiffened. No doubt his neighbors were nubile young things who brought him casseroles and apple pies.

"Why don't you tell me what the great benefits would be?"

"Well." He fitted the front of the drawer to the sides and tapped them together. "Having neighbors is like being on a team. They look out for each other, help out with big chores, take care of the mail or pets when you have to go somewhere."

"This is Montana," she shot back, this time harnessing Jolie who imitated Cody's stunt in climbing up the back cushion. "Security isn't a huge issue. I can hire someone to help with the big chores. I don't have a pet. And I don't go anywhere for anyone to need to pick up my mail. I don't need a team. They're overrated if you ask me."

"Overrated?" The question held disbelief and a touch of insult. "You're talking to a Navy SEAL. Teamwork means the difference between life and death to me."

She suppressed the urge to squirm. "That's different. That's the military. You have to work together."

"We're an elite team of highly trained officers that go into the hottest spots in the world to save strangers, help governments, retrieve sensitive information."

"You're twisting my words." Giving up fighting the two babies, she set them on the floor and gave them toy trucks to play with, and began pacing in front of the fire. "I respect what you do, but I'm not you. Becoming dependent on others is an invitation to heartache."

Flinching as she heard the revealing comment, she turned her back on the room to hide how much of herself she'd just given away.

She heard the drawer slide neatly into place, the clink of tools being replaced.

"Is that what you want for your niece and nephew? A life of isolation and loneliness?"

She whipped around, chest heaving with fierce emotion. "Don't make this about them. They'll have me. They won't ever be alone."

"Rachel." He came around the end of the couch.

"No." Palm raised she stopped him. "You want to help? Fine. Watch the babies. I'm making lunch."

She escaped to the kitchen, which wasn't much of an escape, but as long as she kept her back to the living room she didn't have to see Ford. Or continue the disastrous conversation.

Damn him for making her defend her lifestyle.

Gathering the makings for sandwiches from the refrigerator, she carried the lettuce to the sink to wash.

Who was he to put her on the defensive? So she kept to herself, what was the big deal? She didn't hurt anyone, and this way they didn't hurt her.

Of course Jolie and Cody would have friends. She knew too well how it felt to be an outsider when you craved to belong.

She plunged her hands under the running water and shivered at the icy temperature. She frowned as she realized there was a definite chill in here away from the warmth of the fire.

Propane fueled the heater and the water heater and ran independent of the electricity. The air in here should be comfortable. Getting a bad feeling, she went to check the thermostat, pushing the slider way up to see if it activated the heater.

Nothing happened.

Dread settled low in her stomach. If they lost the propane—and the heat it provided—her plan to keep her distance from Ford would go with it.

CHAPTER FIVE

"DAMN." Irritation and trepidation sounded in the one word.

Noticing Rachel's agitation as she monitored the thermostat, Ford asked, "What's the problem."

Hands on hips, she waited, as if wishful thinking would kick-start the heater. Finally she conceded. "It looks like something has happened to the propane."

Now he understood her worry. Without the heater they'd be restricted to the fireplace for warmth. A huge gust of wind shook the windows, a timely reminder that the storm still raged outside.

"What makes you think so?" he asked though he didn't truly doubt her take on the situation.

"It's cold in the kitchen, and I haven't heard the heater come on in a while."

"Propane turns to vapor when it freezes." Ford joined her by the thermostat. "It could be nothing more than that. Do you have an above ground or below ground tank?"

"Aboveground, but I've never heard of propane freezing and I've lived in these frozen wilds for thirteen years."

He lifted a shoulder, let it drop. "It has to be really cold."

She looked from him to the ice-encased window and back again. "Sullivan, I've known really cold, and never lost the propane."

"Then maybe something fell and broke the connection. I'd better check it out." Ford headed for the closet holding the outdoor gear. He took out the yellow slicker. "Where is the tank?"

"What makes you such an expert on propane?" She demanded from behind him.

Ford dug through the closet, finding gloves he thought might fit, and a warm fleece muffler, thankfully in a simple navy. It was cold enough that he'd have worn a froufrou color, but he wouldn't have liked it.

"If something can be used as an explosive, has ever been used as an explosive, or can be mixed with something to form an explosive, it's my job to know about it."

He surfaced from the closet to find her blocking his path. She scowled, something going on behind those sea-green eyes. But whatever brewed in her thoughts she kept to herself as she answered his question.

"The tank is behind the house. You can see it from my bedroom window." Again she eyed the storm out the front window.

He knew exactly what she saw—nothing but swirling white. There'd been no abatement at all in the weather. If anything, the storm had worsened overnight.

"Let's go see what we can see." Losing the propane wouldn't worry him if it was just him and Rachel, but the babies upped the ante.

In the bedroom he pushed aside her smoky-blue curtains and pulled the cord to lift the mini blinds.

Rachel joined him, using a tissue to clear the condensation from the glass. She pointed to the left. "Over there."

They both looked out on a cloud-darkened world of white on white, with the wicked storm spewing snow and ice through the air.

"It's buried under snow," she said.

He took in the placement, the proximity to the house, the flow and depth of the snowbanks, the visible foliage, making note of the wind direction and velocity. "I see branches between the house and the tank. Do you have something planted there?"

"No. I keep it clear." She shivered. "If it's that cold, maybe you shouldn't be going outside. You don't have the proper gear. That Macintosh isn't going to protect you from the cold and none of my other coats will fit."

"I'll be fine. It shouldn't take more than a few minutes to check things out and decide if there's anything to be done."

Hugging herself, she unconsciously rubbed her upper arms in a warming motion. "It doesn't take long to get frostbite or hypothermia, either. If something happens to you out there, I'm not sure I can get you back to the house by myself. Maybe it's not worth the effort."

He tugged on a short wisp of her blond hair. "You're worried about me."

She ducked her head, pulling away from his touch.

She backed clear up to the bed and abruptly sat when the back of her knees hit the mattress. In a flash she sprung to her feet and headed for the door, leading them away from the intimacy of the bedroom.

Over her shoulder she said, "I may be a loner, but I'm not a monster. Yes, I'm worried, especially if the risk isn't necessary."

He followed her to the end of the hall, propped a shoulder against the wall and watched her pace the living room carpet. For such a tough cookie, she had a marshmallow center.

"Even though I'm the enemy?"

She slanted a glare his way. He probably shouldn't take such pleasure in teasing her, but she riled so easily. Her shows of emotion just pulled him in.

"Yes," she hissed the word then stopped, crossed her arms and cocked a hip, the picture of indignation. "And I don't appreciate being made to feel concern when I'm trying not to like you."

"You might have to give up on that project. I'm a pretty likable guy."

Her eyes narrowed. "You're bossy, nosy and you're planning to take my family away. I think I can resist your questionable wit and charm."

Ouch. That stung more than it should. Time to get back on point.

"We're already low on fuel for electricity, if we lose the propane, too, it's going to get very primitive around here very fast." He notched his head toward the playpen where the twins played. "That would be tough enough if it were just you and me, but with the babies—"

As if cued, Cody's sneeze punctuated Ford's point.

Rachel held up a hand. "I get the picture. I'll go with you."

He started shaking his head before she finished speaking. "Don't even think it. I'll be out and back before you even realize I'm gone."

"Storms are unpredictable. What if something happens to you out there? It's best if we go as a team, like yesterday."

"No. When I went with you to the barn, the babies were asleep. They'll freak out if you leave them alone."

He knew he had her, but she didn't relent until he agreed to a signal system, which made a lot of sense. Every ten minutes she'd yank twice on the snow line and he'd yank back. If he didn't respond, she'd come find him. Then she insisted on giving him one of her large sweatshirts to put under the yellow slicker. He wore extra large so they had to cut out the sleeves to make it fit, but it gave him an added layer of warmth. And the feeling didn't just come from the sweatshirt.

As soon as the door closed behind Ford, time slowed so every minute lasted an eternity.

Rachel tried to convince herself her worry factor would be the same for whoever was out there. The trouble with that was, she was no good at lying to herself. She'd stopped that practice a long time ago.

What insanity gripped her that she suddenly loved the whole world? Okay, that was an exaggeration. But not by far. Not by nearly far enough.

She'd allowed Sullivan to get entirely too close for

comfort. As if by letting the twins into her heart, she'd left a breach for others to slide in, too.

Standing at the sink, her gaze trained on the path Ford would traverse back to the house, she made sandwiches and determined—absolutely—to shore up her defenses.

Just as soon as he got back safely.

He came into view and, breath hitching in relief, she went to the back porch to greet him. He burst through the back door along with a cloud of snow and sleet. She brushed at his head and shoulders as he stamped his feet.

"Good news. The connection is sound. A large tree limb fell, but the tank took the brunt of it." His large shoulders shuddered as his body combated the freezing elements.

"I have a towel and blankets here. Let's get you out of this wet gear." She reached up to help free him of the slicker, but he shook his head.

"I'm going back out. The gauge showed you're at a little over a quarter tank. That's probably why it's freezing. Less mass, and the tree dropped a load of snow and ice on and under the tank. I want to dig it out, create a windbreak to shelter it through the rest of the storm. Where's your shovel?"

"You're half frozen," she protested. "You can't go back out there."

"The exertion will warm me up." He spied her snow shovel in the corner of the porch.

While he gathered it and looked over her other equipment, she rushed to get the coffee she had heating up by the fireplace. She poured a mug and then filled a thermos, dumping in lots of sugar.

She reached the door at the same time he did. He carried a shovel in one hand, an ice hatchet in the other.

"Here—" she thrust the mug at him "—drink this before you go."

She got no argument this time. He drank the coffee in one swallow while she slipped the thermos into the deep pocket of the slicker.

"Be careful," she urged him.

"I will." He wrapped his hands around hers on the mug and squeezed. "Thanks."

The look in his eyes shot right through her, threatening her new resolution. Stepping back, she indicated the door with her head.

"Every ten minutes," she reminded him.

"Two tugs." He confirmed before sliding out of the door, tools in hand.

Rachel's gaze immediately went to the clock marking the time. She needed something to occupy her thoughts or she'd go crazy while she waited. First, check on the babies. Then, more coffee.

She threw another log on the fire before going to the playpen. Jolie slept on her side, a teddy pillowed her head and she still held a toy car clutched in her little fist.

Cody began to cry when he saw her. His nose was running and his eyes looked glazed. He held up his arms and she bent to pick him up.

"Poor tyke. You're not feeling well, are you?" Kissing his forehead, she felt the heat coming off him. "And you're a little warm. Let's get you some medicine. That'll make you feel better."

After cleaning Cody's nose with a tissue, she covered

Jolie with a blanket, checked the time and headed for the medicine cabinet.

She spent the next hour cuddling a fussy Cody, tugging on the snow line and watching for sightings of Ford through her bedroom window. Once he had the tank cleared, the sightings became fewer and fewer, but the heater kicked in after forty-five minutes. So whatever he'd done, it had worked.

Thank goodness. Without the heater, the fireplace would have been their sole source of heat, which would have held them all captive in the living room. Tight quarters for four people, two of whom were at odds with each other.

Ford returned the shovel and ice hatchet to the corner of the porch then pulled off his gloves. When he turned toward the kitchen door, Rachel was there in front of him. Without a word she began helping him out of the wet clothing.

His fingers refused to work the buttons on the slicker. He welcomed her help and took the towel she handed him to dry his neck and hair.

"I've managed to boil enough water to run a warm bath for you." She removed the thermos, placed it on the washer then dragged the yellow plastic garment off his shoulders.

After the roar of the storm outside, the quiet inside struck him as odd and was offset by a low-grade whine. He finally realized the sound came from inside the house. A baby was crying.

"Wh-what's wrong with Cody?" he asked through chattering teeth.

"He's running a low-grade fever. His cold's come back. He'll be all right until we can get you into the tub. Sit." She pushed him into a kitchen chair.

A mug of coffee appeared in his hand, which shook so badly he wrapped the second hand around it as well. The bite of a brandy chaser sent heat rolling through his body.

"Oh my God." He savored the warmth of the brew, the invigorating burn of alcohol. "I think I love you."

She looked up from where she worked on his bootlaces. "Careful, Sullivan. Someone might think you're easy."

"An-anything you want," he stuttered. "Name it, and for another c-cup of this c-coffee it's y-yours."

"Really?" Her eyes turned wistful. "Maybe now is the time to talk about custody."

"Uh-huh." He shook a finger at her. "Truce, remember? No talk of c-custody while we're sn-snowed in."

"Right." Ducking her head so he couldn't see her eyes, she finished removing his boots and socks. Then she refilled his mug, including another shot of brandy. "We'll just put this on account."

She tugged him to his feet and headed him toward the bathroom. "Come on, you can drink that in the tub, you need to get warmed up. I've already put a change of clothes in there for you. The water's lukewarm now, but I can boil more and add it as you start to thaw out. At least until the propane kicks in and we have hot water again."

"Thanks." He stopped at the bathroom door. "I can take it from here."

"Right. Sorry." Color flowed up her neck and into her cheeks. She swung on her heel and crossed the room to a teary-eyed Cody.

A moment later Ford sank into the tub cursing as he lowered his frozen body into the water. His skin came alive with a million stinging prickles. He went from shudders to shivers to chills, which was when he reached for the kettle of hot water.

Sipping from the mug he began to experience a warm sense of well-being. Hearing the heater kick in, he sighed and relaxed back in the tub.

At least his efforts had succeeded. Heck, even if the heater hadn't come back on, the effort would have been worth it. He didn't do idle well. And considering every unoccupied moment allowed guilt-ridden thoughts of Tony's and Crystal's deaths to worm away at his conscience, Ford prayed they'd see a break in the storm soon.

Logically he understood there was no way he could have predicted an earthquake when he purchased the tickets for his friends' vacation. But the bottom line was they'd still be alive if he hadn't bought the tickets, hadn't butted into their business.

And he'd never have met Rachel Adams.

Truthfully he hadn't made any such agreement not to talk custody while the storm held them captive, but he was reluctant to bring it up when they were stuck in such close proximity with each other.

He expected the conversation would get heated, and they may both need fallback room.

The more time he spent with Rachel, the less he wanted to hurt her, but he had to do what was best for the babies.

Ford loved his five brothers, hell, as the youngest, he'd spent his life emulating them or competing for a place among them. It hadn't been good enough to match their efforts, he'd had to do more, do better. He'd earned their respect and a spot on the SEAL team because of the drive and ambition he'd learned early in life. Tony had been a brother of the soul. They'd worked the trenches together, saved each other's hides.

He owed Tony in ways the average person could never understand.

Tony had made it clear he wanted the twins raised with Ford's family, and Ford had had to agree an extended family with aunts, uncles, cousins and a grandmother was a better support team than a lone aunt.

Not to mention San Diego offered cultural, educational and employment opportunities unavailable in Scobey, Montana.

Plus, with the income Ford got from his share in the family jewelry store in addition to his military pay, he had the money to give the babies advantages Rachel wouldn't be able to provide. At least not without touching the life insurance from the loss of their parents.

No matter how he looked at it, he still thought the best plan was for the twins to come home with him. If Rachel wanted to take them occasionally for holidays or vacations, he had no problem working something out with her.

Now he just needed to convince Rachel.

Dressed in jeans and a navy T-shirt and sweater he opened the bathroom door to a prime view of Rachel's heart-shaped butt as she bent to put something in the bottom drawer of her nightstand.

Flush from the tub, the vision of her lush derriere

ignited his blood. The sight of a satin and lace fuchsia thong peeping over the top of her jeans shot him right to boiling point.

Making short work of the hallway and bedroom, he advanced on her so that when she stood and turned it was into his arms. Surprised, her gaze flew up to his. Slowly he cupped her cheek in his left hand, giving her plenty of time to pull away.

"I have to do this," he whispered, "I have to taste you." And lowering his head, he claimed her lips with his.

Oh, yes, so sweet, so hot, she fit against him perfectly ratcheting his blood pressure up another notch. He shifted his head and took the kiss deeper, longer.

Groaning softly, she melted into him and circled his neck with her arms, anchoring herself to his length. She opened her mouth and invited him in, tongues meeting and mating in a sassy dance of give and take.

The intoxicating scents of soap, baby powder and woman wove around him, teasing his senses so he longed for more.

"Closer." Spreading his stance, he pulled her between his legs, pressing her soft breasts to his chest and reaching down with his right hand to trace the flirty line of her thong.

Her breath hitched and a shudder ran through her body, rocking her against him. Murmuring her approval, she tightened her arms around him, and hiked up on her toes aligning her body with his.

He trailed his fingers up to the small of her back and found the softest patch of fine velvet skin. A low moan told him he'd discovered one of her sweet spots. So of course he played his thumb over it again and she went up in flames.

One second she was as lost in the moment as he, the next she'd pushed him away.

"I can't do this." Her voice shook. Taking a step back she tucked her hands behind her, an obvious move to prevent her reaching for him again. "Not with you."

"Rachel." He lifted a hand, needing to touch her, needing to ease the torment in eyes more blue than green.

"No." She sidestepped. "I can't. If you have your way, you're going to take the twins. And that's going to tear me apart. I can't give you this, too."

His hand fell to his side as he watched her walk away.

The next morning the quiet woke Rachel. For a moment she snuggled under her blankets and thought ahead to her day. She'd be done at the clinic by four. Maybe she'd treat herself to dinner at the diner tonight, save time and effort so she could get right to work on her book when she got home.

The sound of a whimper disrupted her thoughts bringing reality rushing back.

The twins.

The storm.

The wolf in hunk's clothing.

Remembering Ford, and the time spent in his arms yesterday, she groaned and buried her head under her pillow. What had she been thinking?

Problem was she hadn't been thinking at all. Tasting, touching, feeling, she'd been doing all of those and more. In fact, her senses had suffered overload at his first touch, and it became all physical after that.

Intensely, mind-blowingly, wonderfully physical.

And it had been sheer insanity.

Really. The man may smell like heaven, but giving into the temptation of his passionate embrace lay the direction of hell.

She'd never forgive herself if she let her libido interfere with her bid for custody. Because make no mistake, he was a warrior, and he'd use every weapon at his disposal to get his way. She'd be a fool not to think that included any perceived affection for him.

Already she'd given too much away by letting him know he possessed the ability to hurt her.

Last night the tension between them could have been cleaved with a hatchet. Cody's fretfulness kept them both busy but only added to the already tense atmosphere. The poor baby just didn't feel good. And she felt for him, but she'd also been grateful for something to focus on besides the blunder of letting go in Ford's arms.

The silence outdoors meant the conversation they'd both avoided could no longer be put off.

About time. In retrospect she wished it had happened before she'd gotten to know him, to like him, to want him. But she'd have to deal with it.

And no time like the present. Tossing aside her pillow, she threw back the blankets and climbed out of bed. She checked on Cody. Because of his restlessness last night, Jolie had slept in the playpen out in the living room with Ford.

Despite a restless night and the whimper she'd just

heard, Cody slept peacefully in his cot. She brushed the back of her fingers over his forehead feeling for a fever. Pleased to find him normal, she tucked the blanket around him and escaped to the bathroom for a shower.

Twenty minutes later she left her room to find Ford and Jolie still asleep. Jolie looked like a little angel. Bare chested with dark stubble and a scowl on his face, Ford looked like a disreputable pirate. Oh, yeah, even sleeping he had that dangerous edge that drew her.

He'd let her sleep in yesterday, so he deserved a sleep in today.

In the kitchen she put on coffee and started pancakes. Jolie woke up first and Rachel snagged her up before she woke Ford. Then she heard Cody through the baby monitor. She changed and dressed both babies then set them up in their high chairs with bowls of pancakes cut into tiny pieces and dusted with powdered sugar.

She glanced into the living room, surprised Ford hadn't stirred yet. She'd heard him cough a couple of times but nothing more. He'd proven to be an early riser. And he didn't strike her as the type to sleep through all the morning activity.

Leaving the twins happily eating their pancakes with their fingers, Rachel slipped into the living room to stand over the couch.

Still sleeping, at some point Ford had pushed the blankets further down his chest so they ringed his waist. He'd also kicked his feet free. This worried her, because even with the heater working, a chill lingered in the air. She wondered if he had a fever? Perhaps he'd caught Cody's cold.

After yesterday morning's lesson in hand-to-hand combat, she knew better than to startle him.

"I'm awake," the words came out in a deep, raspy growl.

"Good, then you won't jump me when I do this." She brushed the backs of her fingers over his forehead and along his cheek, feeling the heat of his skin and the scratch of his beard.

"No promises." He reached up and grabbed her hand, pressing her palm to his cheek. "That feels good."

"You're burning up. How do you feel?"

"I'm fine," he said in the same gravel pit voice. "I don't get sick."

"Uh-huh, Mr. Temperature of 102. I'm going to get you some aspirin, some vitamin C and a cup of tea with Echinacea."

"Don't bother. I just need a shower and I'll be good to go." He sat up and the blankets pooled in his lap.

"No arguments. Think of it as preventative maintenance if it helps. I can't afford for you to be sick when I have two babies to look after."

"I said I'm fine." The denial held a bite.

She propped her hands on her hips. "Fever and grouchy. You'll take what I give you, or we're going to go a few rounds. Then I have pancakes if you're hungry."

"We lost the fire." His glazed blue eyes were angled toward the empty fireplace.

"Yeah. I put the last of the wood on about an hour ago. The good news is that it stopped snowing overnight."

"That's what's different. No wind." He stood and wrapped the blanket around his hips, ran a hand through his disheveled hair. "Good. I'll go out later and fill the wood reservoir."

She sent him a wry glance. "One of us will."

He lifted a dark brow and advanced on her. Suddenly there was nothing debilitating or tame about him. He was hard eyed, hard bodied, hard edged.

With an effort she stood her ground.

"Don't attempt to mother me, dynamite," he breathed against her ear as he walked by her. "That's not a relationship either of us wants."

Wow, she mouthed after he disappeared into the bathroom. Too bad all that male intensity was attached to a totally inappropriate man. The sooner the snow melted and she could send him on his way the better.

The twins belonged with family. She would care and provide for them not out of a sense of duty but out of a sense of love.

Now she just needed to convince Ford.

CHAPTER SIX

FORD placed a piece of wood on the block and cleaved it in two with one swing of the ax. He then quartered the pieces and tossed them into his done pile.

After a morning moping around eating Rachel's cold remedies, he felt well enough—and desperate enough—to escape outside. Cutting wood fit his mood to a T.

Being snowed in gave a man too much time to think, too much time to admire the long, soft curves of his reluctant hostess. To admire her quiet strength and loyalty, her perseverance in the face of uncertainty and her infinite patience when dealing with the twins. Her tolerance of a stranger bent on tearing her world to pieces.

Instead of tasting those luscious lips, instead of dwelling on how he paid for the vacation that had claimed his friends' lives, Ford worked off his frustration and his guilt by swinging an ax.

The very idea of Rachel out here wielding an ax tore his gut to pieces. Not that she wasn't fully capable. That wasn't the point.

Not that it mattered. Because it was none of his business. The only thing that mattered was getting the roads cleared so he and the twins could get on their way to San Diego.

Another log went on the block.

He had arrangements to make. A nanny to hire, a nursery to set up.

Lift and swing.

He always figured he'd wait to start a family until he retired from the team. Now the decision had been taken from him.

But damn. He wasn't ready to hang up his wet suit.

Crack.

Two months ago Tony had signed up for another four years. Ford had planned to do the same when his commission came up in another couple of months.

If the twins' dad could be a SEAL, Ford could be a SEAL.

New log.

All right so that theory held some flaws. Like the fact that Tony hadn't been living with his children. The twins had lived with their mother. And Tony had been in a bad place with Crystal when he'd reenlisted. She'd been adamantly opposed to his SEAL career, which in Ford's opinion had spurred Tony's recommitment for four years.

Lift and swing.

But there was no lying to himself. Ford had disapproved of Tony's decision.

Crash.

Ford believed if you had a family, you owed it to them to be around. Any military position involved risk to some degree. Obviously some more than others.

SEALs were at the extreme end of that category. Which was why he'd been waiting to settle down.

And that brought him full circle.

Guilt, resentment, uncertainty and resolution made for a confusing jumble of emotions spurring on his efforts. In the end it came down to one truth. He owed his friend not only for his solidarity on the battlefield but because Tony would be alive today if Ford hadn't butted into his business.

Ford had a reputation for always following through. With the twins' future on the line, he couldn't fail now.

He stopped, braced the ax handle against his thigh and swiped the back of his wrist over his sweaty brow. The crunch of footsteps heralded the approach of someone.

Rachel was headed his way. Dressed in jeans and a brown parka she moved with athletic grace. In the sun her eyes sparkled more blue than green and the cold weather brought a flush out on her cheeks. Her blond hair contrasted against the fur of her jacket framing her face like a halo.

"Hey, that's quite a pile you have there." She greeted him. "I won't have to chop wood for a month."

"That's the plan." He set a new log on the block. "What about the twins?"

She pulled the baby monitor out of her coat pocket. "They're sleeping."

He nodded toward the monitor she'd tucked back in her pocket. "That's pretty handy."

"Yeah, it's been invaluable. The receptionist at the clinic gave them to me. Everyone's been incredibly kind. When I picked up the twins in San Diego, they gave me one diaper bag with the minimum of essentials included. I had to outfit a nursery from scratch. People at work, my neighbors, they gave me a lot."

"And that's hard for you."

She ducked her head, peeked at him through her lashes. "A little, yeah. I can't help who I am."

"No. We are who we are. Whatever good intentions we have."

Rachel glanced at the pile of wood that would have taken her days to chop. She'd say his good intentions had cost him quite a lot. Remembering his rage of yesterday, she hazarded a guess. "That sounds like guilt talking."

"Yeah." He picked up the ax, but his gaze moved off to the distance.

She went still, touched by his distress. He obviously felt the loss of his friend deeply. Whatever their differences she understood his sorrow. "I'm sorry about your friend."

His grip on the ax handle tightened until his knuckles whitened. "And I'm sorry about your sister. It's hard to believe they're gone."

Rachel swallowed a snowball-size lump. Her relationship with her sister had been so new. In a way, that added to her heartache.

"People say things happen for a reason."

"Eternal optimists." His words had the quality of crushed glass. "People who've never seen the horrific things I have… Death is nothing new to me."

"No, but it sounds like grief is." She gently took the ax from him, set it aside. Clearly she'd hit a raw nerve. "Your job must require a huge amount of skill and bravery, but I imagine in order to see the things you have you'd have had to develop a pretty thick skin."

"Impartiality is necessary, yes. That doesn't mean we don't care." He stood, fists clenched at his sides, his profile a portrait of stubborn pride.

"I can see you do care." No doubt more deeply than he let most people see, which spoke to the level of his torment. "But that's all part of the job. This was different. This was your friends, and there was nothing you could do to save them."

His jaw clenched. "I don't like feeling helpless."

The problem with not interacting with people very often was that she lacked the words to comfort him. So she just spoke from the heart. "We have to think of the babies now, that's what they'd want us to do."

"It's because of me the twins no longer have parents." The confession seemed torn out of him. "How am I supposed to face them every day for the rest of our lives knowing what I cost them?"

"What are you talking about? Tony and Crystal died in an earthquake in Mexico."

"Yeah, and I sent them there. Hell, I paid for the tickets and practically escorted them to their deaths."

He began to pace, snow crunching under the heavy weight of his boots.

She'd never seen him so agitated. "I don't understand."

He drilled her with an anguished glare. "Me. I'm the one who sent them to Mexico. Tony and Crystal were constantly at odds. They never agreed on anything to do with the twins. I thought if they could get away from the problems of everyday life for a while, be together as a family, they might settle some things. Come to an understanding."

"And instead they died."

"Yeah."

And he blamed himself. Which was ridiculous, but he'd brooded about it for so long that simply saying so would have little impact. So that's not what she'd say.

"Wow. No wonder you feel guilty."

He blinked at her, shock in his blue eyes.

"What?" She feigned innocence. "Were you expecting sympathy? This is my sister we're talking about."

"No. Right." He sank down on the chopping block, scrubbed both hands over his face "You're right, I deserve the recrimination."

"Damn straight." She purposely struck a hard note. "This whole thing is your fault."

"Now wait a minute." His head and shoulders went back.

"You owe me." Beginning to circle him, she laid on the guilt. "You owe the twins. Because of you our only family was taken from us. The only honorable thing to do is sign over custody to me so we can keep what's left of our family together."

"The hell you say." He surged to his feet, placing himself directly in her path.

"Hell yes." She propped her hands on her hips and met him chin to chin. "You can also give me the winning numbers for the lottery this week."

His dark brows drew together and he shook his head as if trying to clear his confusion. "What are you talking about now?"

"I'm talking about winning the lottery. The twins and I could use the money. I mean you are psychic right? Otherwise how could you know about the earthquake in Mexico?"

The tension went out of him. "No, I'm not psychic."

She pouted. "No lottery numbers?"

He stepped closer, lifted her chin with the edge of his hand. "No lottery numbers."

"And you're not to blame for Tony and Crystal's deaths?"

"As I have no psychic ability, I guess not." He stared into her eyes, and she saw a lightening of his spirit. "You think you're so smart, don't you?"

"Pretty much." She grinned, then grew serious. "You aren't at fault here, Ford. Don't let it haunt you."

He turned her toward the house, and draping an arm over her shoulders started walking. "We should check on the twins before Cody wakes up and finds something to finger paint with."

"At least I got smart and started separating them for naps."

"Good idea. Yeah, that boy gets into everything, nothing is out of his reach."

"He got you, didn't he?" She giggled and slanted him a look through her lashes. "When you had the kids the other day, he got you."

"I'm not admitting to anything."

"Coward."

"Hey, that there is a fighting word to a SEAL."

She bumped her shoulder into him. "I'm not afraid of you."

"No." He laughed. "You're one tough little cookie." They reached the front of the house. "Thanks for talking trash to me."

She stopped on the first step of the porch, which she'd shoveled clear before going in search of him. Facing Ford now she saw the pain still shadowing his fathomless blue eyes. "But you still feel responsible, don't you?"

"Let's say, you've given me something to think about." His gaze swept her face and he leaned forward.

She saw the kiss coming and lowered her head. "Don't."

"You're a special woman, Rachel Adams." Gently he lifted her chin, and touched her heart by pressing a warm kiss to her cheek. "I wish things could be different."

Ford came awake in an instant. Unmoving he scoped out his environment to determine what had alerted him. The first thing that struck him was the warm weight and sweet scent of the woman in his arms.

He opened his eyes to find he was reclined on the couch, not unusual, as that's where he'd been sleeping, but his bed hadn't been made up and he was still fully clothed. A pity considering the woman cuddled up to him, was—to his disappointment—also fully clothed.

He sure wouldn't mind seeing more of her colorful, sexy lingerie.

A log fell in the fireplace shooting sparks through the grate. He recognized the sound as the one that had awakened him. He should get up, stoke the fire, toss on another log.

He had no intention of moving.

Not while Rachel slept so peacefully against him.

They'd had a busy day between his chopping wood, her shoveling the porch and looking after the kids. After dinner he and Rachel had settled on the couch, a respectful distance apart, and watched Cody and Jolie play in the playpen while discussing the events of the day.

Cody's cold appeared to be on the mend again, and good-natured Jolie put up with his high energy antics with stoic patience. The conversation moved from the kids to films and books, current events and war stories. He told her of the time he'd night-dropped into foreign territory only to get treetopped fifteen feet off the ground. She shared some outrageous animal tales that had him laughing out loud.

It turned out she wrote a syndicated column about animal antics, and had even been offered a book deal she was waiting to hear on.

Yeah, they talked about everything under the sun but what really mattered.

Which was totally out of character for him. He lacked the patience for prevarication.

Tonight had been different.

He'd never spent a more domestic evening with a woman. Didn't usually want to. But tonight, with Rachel, he'd enjoyed a quiet, fun, invigorating and peaceful interlude. She had a biting wit that both challenged and amused him. Even the occasional silences had been comfortable.

During one of those silences they must have fallen asleep. And as the fire died down and the room grew chillier, they'd gravitated together for warmth. Now he was lying with one leg up, one foot on the floor and she lay tucked between him and the back of the couch.

She felt good in his arms, every breath she exhaled whispered over his skin teasing the hair at the opening of his shirt. Her silky hair feathered his cheek and smelled of peach blossoms. And he pillowed their clasped hands, her left in his right, on his stomach.

Giving into temptation he ran his thumb over the petal soft skin of her palm. He longed to touch more of her, all of her. To taste every inch of her and have her ignite in his arms like she did yesterday. Her responsiveness, so sweet and sassy, so genuine, undid him.

The tiny movement of his thumb finally penetrated her subconscious because her hold tightened into a fist around him.

He liked that feeling. He'd hold her close and let tomorrow take care of itself.

Rachel sighed as the tension drained from Ford's body. The even flow of his breathing meant he'd fallen asleep or was close to it.

The stirring of the fire had woken her. How surprising to find herself in Ford's arms. She should have moved, put space and sense between them. Just gotten up and gone to bed.

Instead she'd stolen this time. Illicitly taken advantage of the peace and safety of being held by a strong, gentle man. For these uncounted moments she pretended he didn't want something from her. That he wouldn't be leaving in a matter of days.

For these cherished moments she just lay in the strength of his warm embrace and let herself be.

When he'd started caressing her palm, she'd thought he might try to touch her further, might try to wake her and turn so she was under him.

Her body clenched with need as she imagined welcoming him into her arms and her body.

She inhaled, loving the smell of him, the scents of man and soap with a hint of wood smoke. Oh, how the woman in her wished he'd woken her.

But she couldn't make the move herself. The mother in her couldn't forget the babies even for the length of time it would take to shatter in his arms.

But the woman in her, the one who longed for a man's touch, the one weakened by Ford's thoughtfulness and the tender way he handled the twins, that woman would have succumbed to a midnight seduction.

It wasn't to be.

Sigh. Rachel closed her eyes, content to savor these unplanned hours.

Tomorrow was soon enough for regrets.

The next morning Ford walked the quarter mile down to the main road. The intermittent sunshine yesterday and this morning had started a thaw. He could see patches of the driveway and when he reached the road it had been cleared.

They'd be able to make it into town today to replenish supplies. And the way to San Diego had been opened up.

"I don't know how much longer I'll be," he said into his cell in answer to his older brother's question. "My commander gave me thirty days leave to handle the situation. Now the snow has stopped, I'll be able to get on the road once we resolve the custody issue."

"What's the hold up there? I thought you said she wasn't interested in taking on the twins."

"The picture Crystal painted of her sister was off. Way off. She's already bonded with the kids and she's refusing to sign off on custody."

"So if she's willing and able to take on the task, why don't you let her?"

"Tony made them my responsibility. I can't do my duty by them if they're in Montana and I'm in California."

"I know you don't want to hear it, but you can't do it by jet setting all over the world, either. Maybe they'd be better off in Montana."

"I'm not exactly hopping the globe on pleasure trips. It's my job. And you were singing a different song about responsibility when you took Gabe from Samantha. She was willing and able and you still went after custody."

"Different scenario. Gabe is my son. The twins are not your family."

"They are now. I owe Tony in ways I can't define. I can no more deny his request than I could if something happened to you and Samantha and you left your boys in my care."

"I've always admired your loyalty, little bro. You know we'll support you any way we can."

"Yeah, I know. That's what Tony was counting on." After promising to keep his brother posted, Ford disconnected the call.

He sighed, his breath crystallizing in the air. He and Rachel were long overdue for a conversation on custody. Today he'd get her to sign the papers and tomorrow he and the twins would be on the road.

No more excuses.

As he approached the house he heard a ringing. Sounded like phone service had been restored.

He opened the front door to see Rachel waving her arms in the air and shimmying her hips. A tantalizing strip of creamy flesh showed between her low-cut black jeans and the turquoise sweater that matched her eyes. She danced around the kitchen; making the twins who were strapped into their high chairs, giggle.

"Was that the phone I heard?" he asked.

She whipped around at the sound of his voice and he saw the smile lighting up her face.

"Yes, it was." She shimmied toward him, threw herself into his arms. "The phones are working."

"That is good news. And if you like that…" He waltzed her around the table, twirled her around once and dropped her into a dip. "You'll want to do a jig when you hear the road is clear."

Her eyes laughed up into his. He grinned, taking delight in her happiness. And unable to resist while he had her dipped and at his mercy, he cupped her head in his hand and lowered his head to claim her mouth.

She immediately opened to him. Tightening her arms around him, she returned the kiss with a passion to match his.

Reluctantly he pulled back, brought her upright and twirled her around again.

"Whew." She swayed on her feet, her cheeks burning red. She licked her lips and blinked away the lust glaze from her dazzling eyes. "They want the book."

"Your book on animal manners?" he asked.

"Yes." Excitement made her glow. "That was my agent on the phone. They want my book. The publisher made an official offer."

"Hey." Absurdly proud of her, he swooped her up and swung her around. "That's great news."

She threw her head back and laughed. Joy radiated from her.

The babies shrieked in glee.

Ford realized he'd seen little happiness in her. Passion, resolve, sadness, determination, anger, sorrow. He'd seen all those and more. And certainly love for Cody and Jolie. Yet simple happiness and joy had been missing.

Slowly he lowered her to the floor. When she reached eye level, she sobered. He expected her to push him away as her sense of self-preservation demanded every time he got too close.

She surprised him by throwing her arms around his neck and laying one on him.

The kiss didn't last long but held a punch. Because it was the first overture she'd made to him. When she pulled back, he let her slip the rest of the way to the floor.

She framed his face between her hands. "You made this moment more special by being here. Thank you."

"Hey, this is a big deal." Something bloomed in his chest at her words. Some feel-good emotion that he didn't recognize filled him up. He liked making her feel good even if it meant putting off talking about custody issues. It would take a lesser man than him to spoil her pleasure.

"In fact we need to celebrate. Let me take you to dinner."

"Oh." Flustered, and clearly pleased, a flush added to her glow. But she flittered away, began fussing over the twins. "That's not necessary."

"Of course it is. You deserve a party. And the twins and I are just the ones to give it to you."

She hesitated for another moment, but her excitement couldn't be contained. She grinned. "All right. It's a date."

CHAPTER SEVEN

It's a date. How lame was that?

Rachel surveyed her reflection in the mirrorlike surface of the restaurant door. Looking beyond the little girl in her arms, she saw a woman dressed in a calf length brown suede skirt with brown boots and an ivory sweater under a black leather duster. Too dressy?

Not for a date. Oh God.

Stepping through the door Ford held open, she inhaled the spicy aromas of onion, garlic and tomatoes. Decorated in dark woods and red vinyl with a video arcade and jukebox for entertainment, the Pizza Pit catered to families, sports teams and bored teenagers.

She'd directed Ford to the pizza joint knowing the twins were likely to be excitable after being cooped up for days. And maybe the loud, boisterous crowd, with kids popping up and down and all around, would make it less like a date.

Where had her head been? Answer: In the stratosphere.

Oh, yeah, she'd kept her cool while talking to her agent. But let Ford suggest something simple like a celebratory dinner, and she blew it all out of proportion.

Proximity was the problem.

The enforced intimacy of the last few days gave her subconscious ideas. Working together, sharing the responsibility of the twins, sleeping in each other's arms all played into her dream of having a family.

Ford with his intelligent blue eyes, muscle-ripped body and dangerous edge spoke to every female particle in her. But even more than his skillful fingers and sinful mouth, she responded to his willingness to listen, his patience and generosity, his loyalty and sorrow for his friend and his stubborn sense of duty.

Ideal mating material, or so her subconscious would have her believe.

But it was impossible.

Even if she decided to act on the amazing attraction between them, too many obstacles blocked the goal. He lived a thousand miles away. He was big city, big family, bigger than life. She was small town, family-poor and self-contained. He was a warrior who traveled the world; she was a loner, comfortable in her little corner of Montana.

She followed Ford to a booth not far from the video arcade. Hitching Jolie higher on her hip, Rachel looked around for the high chairs. Spying them by the salad bar, she pointed them out to Ford.

"I'll get them. Here, take Cody." Ford set the boy in her lap next to his sister.

Bouncing the babies on her knees, she watched Ford cross the room, his stride long and graceful. Yum, he looked fine in black jeans, a black T-shirt and black boots.

Out of her league fine.

Heck, he probably had a whole slew of beach bunnies waiting for him back in California. A prime military man with dark good looks and fatal charm, he probably had them lining up and down the pier.

She'd be delusional to think they had a chance in purgatory of being together.

Not only did they not have a future together, he had every intention of tearing her world apart. She'd do well to remember that.

He came back with the high chairs and they got the twins settled. A waitress arrived and Ford ordered the pizza. Pasting on a smile, Rachel tried to keep up her end of the conversation, to get into celebration mode. It was her party after all.

And she did appreciate his gesture. More than she could ever say, but she couldn't pretend any longer.

"It's okay you know," she said after about twenty minutes. "We can talk about the custody plans for the twins."

Clearly startled, he sat back and eyed her. "No." He shook his head. "We're here to celebrate your book. I don't want to spoil it for you."

"I appreciate that, I do." Rather than meet his quizzical gaze, she picked up her discarded straw wrapper. "But I can't sit here and pretend you're not plotting the best way to get my signature on the custody papers so you can pack up Cody and Jolie and truck on back to San Diego."

His features tightened. He almost looked hurt. "Is that what you think I'm doing, sitting here plotting against you?"

"Yes. No. I don't know." Confused, she bought some time by digging in her purse for some crackers to give the twins.

But she'd started this conversation she needed to see it through. "Look, we both know you wouldn't be here with me if not for your interest in the twins, so we might as well deal with the issue."

"I'm in Montana because of the twins." He reached across the table and took her hand. "Tonight I'm with you because I want to be with you."

"Don't." She pulled her hand back, scattering shredded wrapper pieces, her emotions seeming to scatter in the same way. "Please don't say things like that. There's no point. Let's just decide what we're going to do about the twins so we can get on with our lives."

He set his drink aside and leaned forward with concern in his eyes. "Not until I understand what's happening here. Why are you so upset?"

I can't afford to care for you. And I'm afraid it's already too late. But she'd give him too much ammunition by admitting that out loud. "You want to take the twins from me, isn't that reason enough to be upset?"

"I'm not taking them from you," he said carefully. "I'm bringing them into my family. There's a difference."

"They can live with me and still be a part of your family. They can visit you in the summer and on holidays."

"If I thought that would work, I'd go for it in a heartbeat. But we both know that they'd feel like outsiders visiting strangers. My family will embrace them, they'll have aunts and uncles and cousins. They've already played with my brother's boys. They'll have a grandmother. Love will grow and surround them but only by being in the midst of the family."

"I already love them." Her gut clenched in fear. Everything he said made horrible sense. "All of the people you mentioned are the strangers. I'm their family."

"And you can have all the visitations you want. The twins can come here. You can come to San Diego. We'll work it out."

"I don't know how." She glanced at the twins and her heart bloomed with such love she choked up. Swallowing with difficulty she informed Ford, "I won't sign away my rights. I won't. I've thought and thought on how we can make this work because obviously neither of us is going to give up full custody, but nothing makes sense.

"We live too far apart to share custody unless it's for six months at a time. I'd be willing to consider that but honestly I don't think it's best for the babies. It would be disorienting for them when they're this young, especially after losing their parents."

"And when they get older and start school, they'd have to change school every six months." He shook his head. "That's every kid's worst nightmare."

A shadow loomed over the table. Rachel looked up into Sheriff Mitchell's chiseled features. "Evening, folks. Is everything all right here?"

"Sheriff." Ford acknowledged the other man. "I imagine you've been busy these last few days."

"Some." Mitch turned his attention to her, a question in his eyes. "Rachel, how are you doing?"

Rachel sighed; the last thing she needed was a macho

contest between the two men. Summoning patience—
no easy task—she flashed a smile.

"We're fine, Mitch. I hope no one was seriously hurt
by the storm."

"No serious damage, no." His eyes narrowed suspi-
ciously and his gaze shifted from her to Ford and back.

Oops. Maybe she'd overdone the friendliness a bit.

Cody chose that moment to make a grab for Mitch's
shiny steal handcuffs.

"Cody, no," she chided and reached to grab his hand.

Too late. Feeling the pull on his belt, Mitch slapped
his hand down, connecting smartly with Cody's fingers.
Stung, the boy began to cry.

Lightning fast Ford shoved to his feet, shouldering
Mitch aside. "Back off."

"I'm sorry." Mitch held up both hands in a concilia-
tory gesture. "He startled me."

Rachel tensed, ready to jump between the two men
if necessary. But Ford simply nodded and picked up
Cody, quietly murmuring to soothe the distraught boy.

Mitch quickly made his excuses and left.

"I'm going to go run cold water on his fingers." Ford
hefted Cody to his shoulder. "We'll be back in a minute."

Left at the table, Rachel and Jolie looked at each
other. Big eyed, the little girl chewed on a cracker.

"Get used to it, babe," Rachel advised. "Boys never
change."

The pizza arrived just ahead of Ford and Cody's return
to the table. By unspoken agreement they ate in silence.

After a few minutes Jolie began to fidget and whine.
Rachel grabbed the diaper bag and escaped to the rest

room. Besides being wet the baby had developed a rash on her butt and along the waistline of the diaper. Rachel lathered on ointment, finished changing Jolie and rejoined the boys.

She'd barely regained her seat before Ford tossed out a new suggestion.

"What about split custody?"

As soon as he said the words, Ford wanted to pull them back. For so many reasons. In the short time he'd been around the twins he'd observed how they drew strength from each other. His older brothers, Rick and Rett, identical twins, would beat him to a pulp if they'd heard him voice the suggestion. He couldn't conceive of them being parted and the same went for Cody and Jolie.

"Split them up? Like you take Cody and I take Jolie?" She sounded both appalled and fascinated by the prospect. Her gaze went from him to the twins. Without breaking stride she casually removed a paper napkin from Jolie's mouth and handed Cody another piece of crust.

"That would probably be the best division of custody." Why was he pursuing the outrageous option? "What do you think?"

But she was no longer listening.

"Ford." The urgency in her voice caused him to tense. She set her pizza down and nodded toward the video arcade.

He looked over, spotted a pretty brown haired girl about fourteen or fifteen playing a video game. He also noted the young punk, dirty blond hair, oversize clothes, hassling her. The girl tried to walk away, but the boy blocked her retreat.

"I'll take care of it." He slid to the edge of the booth.

"Wait." Rachel's hand on his arm stopped him. "Look."

Another kid—Ford could tell it was the girl's older brother by the resemblance between them—jumped into the fray. He stepped between the punk and the girl, said something that had the punk backing off, then he took the girl's arm and escorted her back to their table.

Ford settled back into the booth. The whole incident lasted only a few minutes. Such a small envelope of time to deliver such a huge emotional impact. How could they possibly separate brother from sister after witnessing such a scene?

He met Rachel's blue-green gaze, saw she'd come to the same conclusion as him. "If I believed in signs, I'd say fate just slapped us with one hell of a lesson."

She arched a delicate brow. "You think?"

"It was a bad idea anyway."

"At last. Something we agree on."

Back at the house, Ford put away the groceries while Rachel got the kids ready for bed. Because she'd been fussy on the way home, Rachel had given Jolie a bottle while she changed Cody and dressed him in his pajamas.

Once he was settled in the crib with his bottle, Rachel reached for Jolie.

"What's wrong, baby doll?" Though she'd taken the bottle the little girl had continued to whine the whole time Rachel had been dealing with Cody. Usually the mellower of the two children, Jolie's distress began to worry Rachel.

Once she'd stripped Jolie down and seen the raw red

welts covering her torso and bottom Rachel's uneasiness turned to apprehension.

"Ford," she called as she inspected the nasty irritation. She felt awful that the baby had suffered all evening. "Oh, poor baby, I'm so sorry. I should have realized something was wrong when I saw the rash earlier."

Ford appeared in the bedroom doorway. "What's up?"

"Jolie has a bad rash. It was only a little red earlier. I thought it was diaper rash. But now she has red welts."

"Let me see." He moved to her side, his features tightening when he saw the livid marks on the girl's delicate skin. "Probably just an allergic reaction. But it looks so bad."

"I want to take her to emergency. Will you stay with Cody?"

He shook his head. "We'll go together."

"There's no need to take Cody out, too. It's better if you stay here with him."

"Forget it." He wore his stubborn expression. "I'm no good at waiting. And I'm not letting you go alone."

"Fine." She could have argued, but she saw the concern under his obstinate façade. And she really would welcome his company. "Let's get going then."

They quickly bundled the babies up and Ford drove them to Daniels Memorial Hospital, where despite Ford's aversion, they spent time waiting. Cody was out like a light in the stroller. Jolie dozed intermittently but the welts obviously bothered her as she woke often. At those times she wanted to be held and walked.

Time dragged, worry escalated, nerves were strung tight, while Rachel lashed herself with self-recriminations. She should have acted sooner. She should have known the rash meant something more.

But no, she'd been too caught up in denying her attraction to Ford and claiming her rights to the twins.

Maybe this was another sign. Maybe Rachel wasn't meant to raise Cody and Jolie.

She'd rather give them up than see them harmed in any way.

"Stop beating yourself up," Ford whispered, his breath warm on her temple as he wrapped his arms around her, helping her to support Jolie's weight. "Kids get rashes, upset stomachs and colds. It's nobody's fault."

Rachel nodded unable to speak for the tears that threatened. His reassurances warmed her icy core. He'd been a rock. For a moment she allowed herself to absorb his strength, to lean just a little.

When they finally got in to see the doctor, a slim woman with blue-black hair and horn-rimmed glasses, they learned Ford had been right. It was an allergic reaction.

Jolie announced her displeasure at being stripped and inspected by screaming at the top of her lungs and trying to twist away. It broke Rachel's heart to have to hold her still for the doctor's examination.

The cries woke Cody. Ford had his hands full keeping the boy from following his sister's example.

"Has Jolie eaten or touched anything new over the past twelve hours?" Dr. Wilcox asked.

"I've racked my brain trying to remember if I fed them something different." Rachel heard the waver in her voice. Determined to keep the tears at bay, she took a deep breath. "We've been snowed in, so we've been eating what we've had on hand. Nothing new."

"It doesn't have to be something she ingested," the doctor clarified. "It could be something applied to her skin or that she's worn. Like soaps, lotions and softeners. It could even be something in the air."

Rachel tried to focus her thoughts. "I'm sorry, Doctor, nothing comes to mind."

"I opened a new laundry detergent when I washed the sheets this morning," Ford said. "She took her nap on those sheets this afternoon."

"Yeah." Rachel wearily pushed her hair back from her face. "I've used that brand before, but not since the twins have been with me."

"You've probably found the culprit, but you should see her pediatrician for allergy tests." The doctor advised. "In the meantime, I'll give her a shot. The welts should go down quickly."

"Thank you, Doctor." Ford settled Cody against his shoulder. "Can I take my family home now?"

A miracle happened on the way home. The twins fell asleep and stayed asleep until Rachel and Ford tucked them into bed. In the playpen. Too late to rewash the sheets tonight, so they'd decided to pile in a couple of blankets for padding and let Cody and Jolie sleep in the living room.

Rachel stood over the playpen watching the babies slumber peacefully. Thank God it hadn't been any more serious than allergies. Even so, she felt as though she'd been put through the spin cycle and hung out to dry.

Ford came out of the bathroom, ready for bed in pajama bottoms and a T-shirt.

"Thank you for coming with me tonight. You made a difficult trip easier."

His gaze ran over her as he rounded the couch. She tucked a strand of hair behind her ear, knowing any glamour she'd managed earlier had long disappeared. She'd already had her turn in the bathroom so she lacked a lick of makeup. And her flannel pajama bottoms and long sleeved thermal underwear were a long way from date material.

Undeterred he stepped right up to her, wrapped a hand around the back of her neck and laid his forehead against hers.

"I'm glad I was there, too." His fingers worked magic on the sensitive skin of her neck. "But you would have handled it. You're one tough lady. You were amazing."

"Oh heavens, Ford. I never want to go through that again." Too weak to resist the lure of his comfort and strength, she relaxed against him.

"Me, neither." He ran his hands down the backs of her arms until his fingers tangled with hers then he stepped back pulling her with him. "You've had a tough day. Come lie down. I want to hold you."

"Oh. I shouldn't." She let him go until their arms were stretched full-length, but her resistance stopped there. When he continued walking she followed step for step. Sleeping in his arms sounded like heaven. But oh, she shouldn't. "You said it yourself, I'm tough. I don't need to be held."

"I do." He drew her down to the couch and into his arms. "Just for a while. Hold me."

When he lay back and took her with him, she let him. And oh it felt so good, so right to lie in his arms. She snuggled her cheek over his heart, sighed and closed her eyes.

"All right. But just for a little while."

CHAPTER EIGHT

FOR the second day in a row Rachel awoke on the couch alone. How Ford had managed to slide away without waking her she didn't know. The man had skills.

Not least of which was sneaking past her defenses.

The harder she tried to create distance between them, the closer he seemed to get. He'd claimed to be a likable guy and she had to agree. Damn it.

He'd be much easier to resist if he were a selfish jerk, which considering his insistence on taking the twins should have qualified him hands down. Unfortunately he carried his weight and more with household chores. His patience and gentleness with the twins never wavered. Heck, he even changed diapers without complaining.

His loyalty and sense of duty were the biggest bane of her life. And confirmed the honor his commanding officer proclaimed he had in spades.

He made her think, he made her laugh, he made her want.

But she couldn't—wouldn't—give in to the insanity of falling for him. Of all the mistakes she could make, that would be the biggest.

Hearing giggles from the kitchen motivated her to get up and get going. She hopped into the shower, brushed her teeth, and then dressed in jeans and a flannel shirt over a navy T-shirt.

In the kitchen she found a fresh pot of coffee, Ford kicked back reading the paper, and the twins covered from the waist up in applesauce as they pounded the trays of their high chairs with spoons. The bigger the mess they made the more they giggled.

Rachel shook her head and moved to pour herself a cup of coffee. She leaned back against the counter and sipped.

"Having fun?"

Ford lowered the paper far enough to meet her gaze. "Good morning."

Approval shone in his eyes even after his gaze had swept her from head to foot. Here she stood without a lick of makeup, and he'd made her feel as if he'd never seen a more beautiful sight in the morning.

The man had to go, and the sooner the better.

Before she did something foolish, like do more than sleep in his arms.

Like fall in love.

She hitched her chin toward the twins. "They're dangerous with those spoons. You know they haven't learned to feed themselves yet."

He folded the paper and set it on the table then flicked a glance at Cody and Jolie. "It'll wash off. And they won't learn if they don't try."

"Huh. It's good to hear them laughing."

"Yes. The welts are down on Jolie. She's looking

much better." He got up and punched some numbers on the microwave. Next he dropped bread in the toaster. "Sit down, I made breakfast."

"You spoil me." She took a seat at the table just as he set down a plate of scrambled eggs and smoked sausage.

"You make that sound like a bad thing." He went back to the counter for the toast.

"It is. I'm used to doing things for myself. I prefer it that way."

"Maybe that's why I like doing things for you." He sat down and pushed a plate of buttered toast toward her. "Because it's not expected."

"Huh." She flashed him an exasperated glare.

He grinned. "Eat up. I have a surprise for you."

She lifted her brows at him. "All this and a surprise, too? Are you sure you don't want to quit the Navy and move to Montana?"

The levity left his expression and his eyes turned pensive. "My brother thinks I should give up the SEALs now that I'm guardian of the twins."

"And you're not ready to?"

"Honestly? I don't know. My current commission is up in a couple of months, so I don't have long to think about it. I do know I want it to be my decision. Not something forced on me by circumstances or told to me by my brother."

"That would be ideal, wouldn't it? If outside influences and well intentioned advice didn't play a part in our decisions."

The exasperation boomeranged back to her. "Very funny."

"You're just upset because you have to think about this before you were ready to. Let me ask you this, does your brother expect you to quit because he voiced an opinion?"

"No, if anything, he'd expect the reverse."

"Why's that, because you're the youngest of six and you've been bucking the system since the day you learned to say no?"

His eyes narrowed in speculation. "How do you know that about me?"

"Please, I've known you what, a week? And I already know you can find Ford as a synonym for stubborn in a thesaurus. You haven't accepted no for an answer since you got here and when you have compromised, it's been on your terms." She reached for the grape jelly for her last piece of toast. "Your brothers must know you are your own man."

"Yeah, we all know that about each other." He reached over, took her toast, bit the end off and handed it back to her.

A smear of jelly clung to the corner of his mouth. Rachel bit her lip to keep from acting on the impulse to lean over and lick the sweet treat from his skin. Instead she sank her teeth into the same end of the bread he had and lectured herself on forgetting the physical attraction to concentrate on the conversation.

"So the decision is yours to make. Whether you allow the circumstances to influence you or not is up to you."

He looked at her for a long moment, his expression giving nothing away.

"You're not going to suggest you keep custody of

the twins so I can re-up as a SEAL? We both know you want to."

"You mean because it makes perfect sense for me to take the kids while you pursue your career?"

Yes, it had occurred to her. And yes, she wanted to keep the twins. But begging would weaken her position. She'd learned that lesson too well, and too early in life to forget it when it mattered the most.

"No, I'm not going to suggest that. You're smart enough to come up with it on your own."

"Right. My brother mentioned the arrangements for Tony and Crystal's memorial service were set for the week before Thanksgiving. Will you come?"

"Your family made arrangements for Crystal?" The thoughtfulness of the gesture staggered her.

"It's what I thought you'd like. If you prefer to make other arrangements, I can let my brother know."

"No. No. She'd want to share this last rite with Tony. Of course I'll come."

Jolie called for her attention, breaking the growing tension.

"Good morning, baby. You're feeling better aren't you? I'm so glad." Rachel grabbed a napkin and swiped at Jolie's face. "But oh my. Uncle Ford let you make one big mess, didn't he?"

"Da na da." Cody pointed his dripping spoon toward Ford and grinned showing two bottom teeth.

Rachel's gaze met Ford's. He looked shell-shocked for a moment before shutting off all expression.

She knew how he felt. The first time she thought the twins called her mama both broke her heart and mended it back all at the same time. The incongruity along with the inherent acceptance struck right to the core of you. And revived the sorrow of loss all over again.

"Just coincidence." She crossed her arms over her chest. "They don't know what they're saying yet." But she knew the day wasn't far away.

Thinking of Ford being called daddy made her gut clutch. She loved the idea the twins were starting to adjust, that they felt loved enough to accept her and Ford in their parents' stead. But that meant they would be hurt again by whatever custody settlement she and Ford decided on.

Sometimes life just sucked.

"Hey, bud, let's get you cleaned." Ford reached for a dish towel and wrapped it around Cody. Ford carefully didn't look at Rachel when he asked, "Bath?"

Rachel stepped out onto the porch, a bundled up Cody riding her hip, to find old Mr. Brown from next door sitting on the perch of a shiny red sleigh drawn by a well-groomed, gray speckled horse.

"Ms. Adams," he greeted her with a huge grin and a tip of his red plaid hat. "Beautiful day for a ride."

"Mr. Brown." Determined to be neighborly she answered his good cheer with a smile. "I hope you and Mrs. Brown survived the storm in tact."

"What ya say there? Sorry lass, don't hear as good as I used to."

Rachel walked to the top of the stairs and, raising her voice. repeated her question.

"That we did, young lady. The Mrs., though, she

caught a chill. I've been feeding her chicken gravy and biscuits, so she should be feeling better right soon."

"Chicken gravy and biscuits?"

"Yeah, yeah. Chicken noodle soup is more than an old wives' tale. It really works to help cure a cold. Don't know how to make chicken noodle soup, but I can make chicken gravy and biscuits. I figure it's close enough."

"I'm sure she appreciates your efforts." Rachel didn't know how well his heavy meal worked on the cold but at least it wouldn't hurt the woman. Rachel made a note to send some Echinacea tea home with him.

"Oh, the Mrs. always appreciates my efforts," he said and winked.

"Mr. Brown." Rachel chided him.

He cackled, pleased to get a rise out of her.

"Here now, that little guy wants to come say hello to Betsy. You bring him on down here." Spry for a man in his sixties, he hopped to the ground. He took Cody from her to gently instruct the little boy on how to pet the horse.

"I had Betsy out for a ride this morning. Met your young man down by the road. He thought you and the little ones might like to get out of the house and go for a ride."

Her "young man" was simply diabolical.

"Yes, I think we'll all enjoy a trip through the snow. This is a beautiful sleigh."

"She is a beauty isn't she?" He beamed. "I got it out yesterday to get it cleaned up and ready for Santa."

She blinked at him. "Santa?"

"Yeah, I've driven Santa's sleigh in the Thanksgiving Day parade for the last eight years. I'm sure you've seen it."

She shook her head. "I'm not much for crowds. I don't go to parades."

He laughed. "Lass, there are more people in the parade than watching it. The little ones would enjoy it."

Ford joined them saving her from having to reply. But Mr. Brown had a point. From now on she had to think beyond her own comfort zone to accommodate the twins.

"John, thanks for giving us a ride." Ford shifted Jolie to shake hands with Mr. Brown. "The kids are going to love it."

"My pleasure. Let's get you folks loaded up."

The men continued to exchange pleasantries while they all got settled, Mr. Brown on the perch, Rachel and Ford with the twins between them in the back.

And then they were off, gliding over pristine snow to the merry jingle of bells. Tucked beneath blankets, the cool air invigorated rather than chilled.

The twins took in everything red cheeked and bright eyed. Rachel figured she looked much the same. It was beautiful and fun. And never before had anyone ever done anything so special for her. For the twins, too, of course, but she knew Ford had done this mostly for her.

The scenery shimmered into crystal brilliance as moisture swelled in her eyes.

"Hey." Ford cupped the back of her neck and ran his thumb over her cheek. His touch felt especially warm against her wind-chilled skin. "Are you crying?"

"No, of course not." She blinked away the tears. "It's just the wind."

"It's more than the wind." He insisted. "Talk to me,

Rachel. This was meant to be a treat, to make you happy not sad."

"I am happy." She assured him. "This is wonderful. The twins are loving it."

"And you? Are you loving it?" The intensity in his blue eyes convinced her the answer really mattered to him.

"I am," she confirmed. Hearing the huskiness in her voice, she cleared her throat, met his gaze. "Thank you for arranging this adventure. Nobody's ever done anything like this for me."

"You mean planned a surprise for you?" He gently tugged on a lock of her hair.

"That, or done something for me just because they thought I'd enjoy it." The confession didn't come easily. She didn't talk about her childhood, ever. But Ford had shared his guilt and sorrow with her and he'd put together this lovely surprise. He deserved some consideration from her.

"I had a strict upbringing." Okay, slight understatement there.

"Is that why you left home so young?" he asked.

She hesitated, glanced at Mr. Brown. He hadn't tried to participate in the conversation. His poor hearing along with the cheerful bells ensured their privacy.

"Yeah, and because I learned I wasn't my father's daughter." Funny, she'd thought the words would be harder to say. But here, with Ford, she said them for the first time and felt lighter.

"Wow. Heavy. How'd you find out?"

"My mother told me. I had to get a job when I was fourteen to help with expenses. My expenses, as it turned out. I didn't get an allowance, but I got to keep part of my paycheck. My senior year of high school, I wanted to buy a car. I'd saved my money. It wasn't hard considering I was never allowed to do anything.

"Mom said I'd need the money when I graduated because I'd no longer be welcome to live with them. I was shocked. That's when she told me she'd been pregnant when she'd married my dad. She'd lied and told him I was his. He'd found out and their marriage survived the truth, but he never accepted me, never loved me."

"Your mom sacrificed you for her own comfort." Ford cut to the heart of her past, the harsh edge in his tone criticizing her mother's choices. Too bad she had no excuses for her mom.

"I didn't wait to graduate. I packed up and left the next day. I bought a one-way ticket to Scobey and started a new life."

"It must have been difficult." The simple sympathy almost undid her.

"It was a relief to be free. I never felt loved in that house. Except by Crystal." She looked down at her hands clasped together in her lap. "Why do you suppose she misled Tony about me?"

He caught her chin and turned her head to face him. Bending, he sealed his warm mouth over hers, telling her with lips, teeth and tongue of his admiration and affection. Sealing the kiss with his lips, he pulled back.

"Whatever her reasons, you have nothing to be ashamed of. You're a strong woman who's made a good life from a bad beginning."

"Thank you." She cupped his cheek in her hand and

showed her gratitude with a soft kiss in return. "I know that's true, but it's easy to believe the worst when someone you love bad-mouths you."

"I can only speculate. Tony didn't talk much about his relationship with Crystal, but I know it was tempestuous. They loved each other, but they weren't compatible."

Rachel recalled the e-mails where Crystal poured out her fears of losing Tony. She'd despised that he was a SEAL. "I know she hated it when Tony went out of the country."

"Yeah, that was tough on Tony. Being a SEAL defined who he was. His parents were alcoholics and they really did a job on his self-esteem. He was one of the best men I knew, but he had no sense of self-worth except on the job."

"I told her she needed to make peace with his job or let him go. It wasn't fair for her to impose her fears on him."

Not that Rachel was an expert on relationships, but one lesson she'd learned, and learned well, was you couldn't make someone love you. And if you weren't true to yourself, you'd have nothing to hold on to when you realized the truth.

Ford nodded his agreement. "They did break up for a while before she found out she was pregnant."

"Really? I didn't hear from her for several months. Then she called to tell me she was expecting a baby. She was so happy. I thought she'd made her peace. Now I realize she probably just stopped sharing her fears with me."

"The pregnancy did bring them closer. Until Tony made out his will. I knew there was no love lost between him and his parents, which is why I agreed when he asked me to watch over the kids if anything ever happened to him."

He lifted his hand to cover hers. "Crystal was young, only twenty-one. She was in love with a man she didn't really understand and couldn't control. I've been thinking about it and I think part of it was my fault."

"How could that be?"

"She didn't like that Tony named a guardian without consulting her. She didn't like that he chose a bachelor, hated that it was another SEAL. I was her worst nightmare."

"Mustang, wild and free." Rachel began to see what motivated her sister's actions. She still didn't like it, but a mother's concern accounted for a lot.

"Pretty much." Ford agreed. "My guess is she set up her own will listing you as guardian then played up the negative aspect of your life to teach Tony a lesson, both for leaving her out of the process and for choosing an inappropriate guardian. Being so young, she probably figured they had plenty of time to deal with the whole issue. It's the only reason I can think of."

She gave him a sad half smile. "I guess we didn't get as close as I thought."

The twins objected to being squeezed between them by squirming and pushing against them. When Rachel settled back into her corner, Jolie pulled on Rachel's sleeve and hauled herself to her feet. The better view and the wind in Jolie's face made her grin and clap her hands. Soon Cody stood next to her.

Turning to better anchor Jolie in place, Rachel noted

Ford did the same with Cody and they were suddenly facing each other. Rachel felt as if they were in an oversize snow globe, an intimate cocoon with the beauty of a winter wonderland passing in the background.

Too bad the intensity of the conversation didn't match the splendor of the scenery.

Jolie laid her head on Rachel's shoulder. The excitement had worn her out. As always the acceptance and trust of Jolie's slight weight resting against Rachel sent warmth flooding through her. She settled the sleepy baby in her lap and wished Jolie could have grown up knowing her mother.

"Poor Crystal and Tony, they just wanted to take care of their kids. But instead of working together they worked against each other and didn't resolve anything."

"That would be my take." Ford stopped Cody from climbing into Rachel's lap along with his sister. He lifted Cody into his lap instead. "Hey, buddy. Let's get you warmed up." Ford tucked a blanket around the boy.

"And now here we are," Rachel said, "trying to make sense of their mess. At least Tony's parents are out of the picture."

"For now anyway."

That sounded ominous. "What's that mean?"

"It means if we don't work out a solid home situation for the twins, it'll leave room for Tony's parents to sue for custody."

"But they couldn't win." Her heart sank at the thought of the twins in the hands of the abusive couple. "A court's not going to give custody of small children to alcoholics."

Ford shrugged, his expression grimmer than she'd ever seen it. "They're closet drinkers. As an established couple making decent wages living in a nice neighborhood, the courts may find them eminently better than two single people living a thousand miles apart splitting or sharing custody."

"Oh my God." Put like that their chances did sound bad. "Why didn't you mention this before?"

"Because I didn't intend to split or share custody. I intended to take the twins and surround them with the strength and support of my family."

Her heart latched onto one word. "Intended? Does that mean you no longer have that intention?"

"It means I want you to move to San Diego."

CHAPTER NINE

THE cold must be getting to her because she thought he'd just asked her to move to California.

She looked askance at him and pounded the side of her head a couple of times. "I don't think I heard right. Did you just say move to San Diego?"

"Yeah, think about it. It makes perfect sense."

"It makes no sense whatsoever."

His somber expression didn't lighten. "I'm serious."

"No." The cold must be getting to him, too. "You're delusional."

"That's a knee-jerk reaction. Don't dismiss the idea without thinking about it."

"What's to think about? This is my home."

"No, it's where your house is." He delivered the harsh decree with utmost gentleness. "You've built a life here, but by your own admission you've isolated yourself from the community. I haven't heard you mention another woman's name besides Crystal. Who's your best friend?"

Ouch. The question cut deep.

And then her spinning thoughts spit out the words, you are.

The instinctive response irritated her almost as much as his question. And how revealing that in the short time she'd known him, she'd become closer to him than people she'd known for thirteen years.

"Just because I prefer my own company doesn't mean I don't have c-connections here." Hating the break in her voice, she buried her nose in Jolie's soft brown curls.

Ford slid closer. Once again she felt the tensile strength of his hand on her neck. Massaging soothingly, he melted her.

"I'm not suggesting there won't be sacrifices, but this could be the solution to our custody dilemma. You're going to have to move anyway. The three of you won't fit in a one-bedroom house for long. You can write anywhere, and there are bound to be plenty of opportunities to work with animals in San Diego.

"Look, you don't have to make a decision right now. You're coming to California for the memorial service, right? I'm just asking you to keep an open mind. Check out the area and consider staying."

Mr. Brown pulled the sleigh to a stop in front of Rachel's house effectively ending the conversation. Between expressing her appreciation to Mr. Brown, running inside for the Echinacea tea for Mrs. Brown and getting the kids inside and settled down for their afternoon naps, Rachel kept busy.

But for all the activity, her mind revved around one thing. The possibility of moving to California.

But it wasn't the practicalities that snagged her attention. It wasn't even the fear of leaving the comfort and safety of small town Scobey for the cosmopolitan metropolis of San Diego.

Although those concerns niggled at her psyche, what occupied her mind was being so close to Ford. She'd known him a week and already her emotions were way too involved. And, much as she'd fought it, not at all platonic.

The attraction went both ways but that only made the situation more dangerous.

If it had been anyone other than Ford, she'd seriously contemplate jumping his fine bod and riding the electric blaze until it caught fire or fizzled out. But a fling with her co-guardian? Not a smart move.

It opened up too many options for sticky relations down the line.

Moving across country may well solve their custody issues, but could she live so near him and just be friends? Could she watch him date other women, cut their wood, surprise them with sleigh rides and still maintain a personal relationship for the twins' sake?

The part of her that had learned not to trust emotions saw no problems ahead. But every other feminine instinct she possessed shouted out a warning.

And were his motives for asking strictly to make things easier with the twins? Or did he have a more personal reason for wanting her in California? He hadn't inferred any kind of intimate relationship in his request.

Yet he hadn't exactly kept his hands to himself, either.

After taking all that angst into account, none of it really counted. The twins mattered. What was best for them mattered.

Like her, they'd fallen under Ford's charming spell.

If a resolution to the custody issue let her keep the twins and allowed them to be closer to Ford, how could she deny them the opportunity?

Ford wanted her to think about moving? Ha, she'd be lucky if she could focus on anything else.

A cheerful fire crackled in the hearth. Soft jazz played in the background. A nice red wine was breathing on the counter. The furniture had been pushed back, and Ford had spread a plush blanket on the carpet in front of the fire. Rachel tossed down several overstuffed pillows.

A more romantic scene would be hard to find.

Until Rachel sprinkled the area with a handful of plastic toys.

Sighing, Ford lifted Cody from the playpen and set him in the middle of the blanket. He shouldn't be thinking about seduction anyway.

Rachel set Jolie next to her brother and then settled against one of the big pillows. Pretty in a soft pink sweater topping black jeans, she looked sexy as hell. She glowed in the flicker of the fire, her appeal due more to good health and hair that looked like she'd just climbed out of bed than makeup or hair gel.

On this, his last night in Montana, they'd decided on a fireside picnic. The twins loved it when he and Rachel got down on the floor and played with them. He wanted tonight to be fun and carefree.

Too bad he didn't feel in the least lighthearted.

A week ago he'd thought he'd come in, save Tony's kids from the clutches of their evil aunt and shoot back to San Diego where he'd leave them in the capable care of his family. Now he dreaded walking out the door, dreaded leaving Rachel and the twins behind.

"You're sure you'll be all right traveling with both kids? They're going to be quite a handful." He dropped to the ground and stretched out.

A flash of panic came and went in her incredibly expressive eyes. "Don't remind me or I may change my mind. I love them so much even though I've only had them a couple of weeks. And they're just two little babies, but they're a lot of work." She cringed. "I mean—"

He held up a hand, shook his head. "I've only been here a week." A ball bounced off him and he rolled it back to Cody, enjoyed the boy's laugh. "I understand too well."

"The idea of traveling with two babies is daunting, but the flight's only a few hours. And you'll be waiting at the other end."

"Right, piece of cake. You'll be in San Diego before you know it."

Again the flash of panic reached her eyes. To distract her, Ford offered to get their dinner, a fragrant stew she'd been slow cooking all day. She waved him off and immediately jumped up to get the meal.

Ford winked at Cody who'd pulled himself up to lean against Ford. "Works every time. Keep it between us men."

He rewarded Cody's cooperation with a cookie and handed one to Jolie. They'd already eaten pasta and peaches. The cookies were a treat that Rachel had set within reach to keep the kids occupied while the two of them ate.

She came back with two steaming bowls of stew, a

plate piled high with golden brown biscuits and two glasses of wine. Setting the tray on the ottoman coffee table, she handed him a cloth napkin.

"Sit." He told her. "You did the rest. I'll serve you."

"Okay." She sank down across from him and smiled as he fussed over her dinner.

He liked doing things for her. Talking to her. Looking at her.

They finished the stew, and the wine. He polished off the biscuits and a couple of cookies. All the while chatting and watching the twins play.

Time flew when he wanted each moment to stretch into forever. There was a lesson in relativity for you. Put him in the middle of a nest of terrorists and every minute lasted an hour. Yet tonight, in a room with a lovely, intelligent, witty woman playing with his delightful wards and every hour rushed by in a blink.

He felt his departure looming closer and closer.

Jolie crawled over and he helped her to climb up. Leaning forward she gave him an openmouthed kiss.

"Ah, baby." He wrapped her in a hug, kissing her soft curls. She laid her head on his shoulder breaking his heart with her love and trust.

In the next moment she wiggled to be set free. He sat up and held her fingers as she walked to Rachel who held her arms up ready for the trade off.

Suddenly Jolie let go and took two steps on her own straight into Rachel's arms.

"Oh my God, Ford," Rachel exclaimed. "She walked. Did you see her? Jolie walked. How smart you are." She covered the baby's face in kisses.

"I sure did." Ford clapped to show his pride in the girl. "Isn't she clever."

Cody, seated on the blanket between Ford and the fireplace, clapped, too. And added a gleeful shriek for good measure. He didn't understand what happened, but he felt the excitement.

Proud of herself, Jolie pushed away and turned to face Ford wanting to repeat her new trick.

Grinning ear to ear, he held out his arms and wiggled his fingers. "Come on, baby, come to Ford."

She toddled three steps and he grabbed her before she fell. The game continued with love and laughter. Cody wanted to take his turn, too. He couldn't quite keep his balance, but Ford shared a look with Rachel, they both knew it wouldn't be long.

Finally Rachel called for bedtime. Working together he and Rachel made short work of bathing, changing and tucking the two exhausted babies into their crib. They were asleep before Ford and Rachel backed out of the room.

Back in front of the fire, Ford handed Rachel a second glass of wine. He tapped his rim against hers. "To Jolie."

"I'm glad you were here to share the moment." She sipped around a grin.

"Me, too."

"You're wonderful with the kids." She leaned back against a pillow. "How come some lucky girl hasn't dragged you down the aisle?"

He shrugged. "There have been some special women along the way. But I wasn't ready to give up being a SEAL and they weren't willing to wait."

"No room for compromise? Then it must not have been love."

He cocked a brow. "Don't look now, but your cynicism is showing. You say that like you don't believe in love."

"Hard to believe in something you've never known." She turned her gaze to the fire but not before he saw the wistfulness in the aqua depths.

"You're right, I didn't love them enough to be tempted to break my rule."

She eyed him over her wineglass. "What rule is that?"

"My friends call it Mustang's rule. Basically I've never thought it would be fair to commit to a permanent relationship while I'm a SEAL. Not only for the woman, but for me. I'm not the type to forget my family back home, which is necessary in order to get the job done."

"I suppose it's good to know yourself so well. Being a SEAL obviously means a lot to you."

The admiration in her voice bolstered his confidence. Naturally reticent, the closeness they'd developed encouraged him to share feelings he usually kept hidden.

"Yeah, it does. It means I'm one of the best."

"No," she waved her wineglass back and forth in a negative gesture, "the training did that. What does the job mean to you?"

Nobody had ever made such a distinction before. He had to think for a moment.

"Justice."

"Justice? In what way?"

"There's a lot wrong in the world. A lot of evil people doing evil deeds. As a SEAL, I make a difference. It's not black and white. But nothing ever is."

"You fight for those who can't fight for themselves."
She toasted him. "Commendable. But you won't be a
SEAL forever. What comes next?"

So intense. Her skin looked translucent in the golden
glow of the fire. He traced the gentle curve of her cheek.
"You ask some tough questions."

"They're only tough if you don't have the answers."

"Ouch." The woman pulled no punches.

She turned on her side to face him. Her fingers found
his on the blanket between them. She traced and played,
warming him with her touch.

"Have you thought about training?" She suggested.
"I think you'd be very good as an instructor."

His commander had asked the same question. Disdain
curled the corner of Ford's lip. "Haven't you ever heard
the expression those that can do, and those that can't
teach? In this case, those that no longer can, teach."

"You don't believe that." But after meeting his gaze
straight on, she changed her tune. "I see you do. Why?
Do you have so little respect for those who trained you?"

Her question took him back to BUDS training, to the
extreme tests of endurance, lack of sleep and larger than
life trainers. He hadn't doubted their skill at the time,
hadn't dared. So why did he now?

Because he didn't feel up to the challenge? Or
because others would know he could no longer handle
the heat of active duty?

"Hum." The low sound in her throat shouted a
warning: facetious comment coming. "Surprising you
got to be the best with such inferior teachers." She laced
her fingers through his, anchoring him even as she chal-

lenged him. "Maybe your condescension isn't so much what you believe, but what you think others will believe."

How did she do that, zero right in on the heart of his fears before he'd even recognized them himself?

"You mean disparaging the job is a self-defense against considering it as an option for the future. The great subconscious at work."

"It makes sense. You're a man of action obviously torn about settling down. What better way to put off a decision than to find something wrong with your choices?"

He flopped down on his back. Self-examination was a bitch. "So basically, I'm being a wimp."

"Not at all." She crawled over so she looked into his eyes, compassion rained down on him. "It just proves you're human like the rest of us."

She traced the rasp of his beard with a curved knuckle. For a sassy, standoffish loner, she'd become quite the toucher. He liked it.

"I'm pretty sure they don't let wimps in the SEALs."

He grinned. "Damn straight. You're right about one thing. It's wrong to disrespect my trainers. They put us through hell, but we were ready when we hit the field."

The concern in her eyes lingered. "Just remember if you decide to pursue training. When you were ready, the instructors let you go. What happens after that belongs in the field not in your conscious."

"Heavens." She was talking about his guilt over buying the trip for Tony. In this she was wrong. They weren't the same thing at all. SEALs were ready for anything and everything when they hit the ground. They planned and trained for best and worst case scenarios.

Tony hadn't been prepared, his training hadn't helped him because he couldn't know an earthquake was going to hit. He couldn't save himself or Crystal because an earthquake provided no warning before raining down horrific destruction.

Ford ran his hands over his face, trying to scrub away the senseless helplessness. *Tony couldn't have known an earthquake was going to hit.* So how could Ford?

If only letting go of his guilt was that easy.

He looped his arm around Rachel, tucked her into his side. "How did you get to be so wise?"

"I don't know about wise." She placed her hand on his chest, and he covered it with his, pressing her palm over his heart. "I admit I'm a loner. But I'm also an observer. People and animals, we're not so different. We give love and loyalty until we learn the pain of rejection, we fight when cornered, and we shy away from what scares or hurts us."

Maybe that was Ford's problem, he'd never run scared. From the day he was born sixth in a family of sons, he'd been fighting for his place in the world. Which explained why he didn't recognize his subconscious at work.

And why he kept finding ways to put his hands on Rachel.

He understood the sense in keeping their interaction platonic. But in learning to fight for what he wanted, he pretty much got what he aimed for. Everything in him demanded more than the feel of her in his arms.

He desired all of her, and not for the sake of the twins.

When he got her to San Diego, she'd be his. And he wouldn't let her go until she agreed to stay.

CHAPTER TEN

A NEW storm came in delaying Rachel's flight by a day and a half. She fretted all the way to San Diego. Thankfully the twins behaved beautifully because nothing else was going as planned.

Because of the delay they'd have to go straight to the memorial service. There'd be no time, or place, to change once she arrived so Rachel wore the new black dress she'd bought onto the plane. She counted it a blessing she'd be attending in wrinkled splendor. Better that than not attend at all, which had been her worst and most likely fear until the wheels of the aircraft had left the tarmac.

The past week had been harder than Rachel had ever anticipated. The kids missed Ford, especially Cody. The two had really bonded over the last week. What Rachel hadn't expected was that *she* was missing Ford just as much.

How quickly she'd become accustomed to his presence, his help, his touch.

I wasn't that she hadn't had contact with him. She'd talked to him on the phone every day, sometimes more than once. And Ford had talked to the twins. Okay, so the kids couldn't talk and they usually tired of the conversation long before the adults disconnected, but she and Ford had had things to discuss, travel arrangements to make. They'd done a lot by e-mail but it wasn't the same.

Not the same as hearing his voice, his laugh, his concerns. She liked that he felt able to talk to her. Especially since she'd become a regular Chatty Cathy around him.

This week had taught her two things. One, she loved Cody and Jolie too much not to be a part of their lives. Whatever it took, she'd find a way to retain custody. And two, she was already way too attached to Ford. If she were smart, she'd forget her promise to think about moving to California and hotfoot it back to Montana as fast as possible.

Two insights and both put her heart on the line. Too bad they were at complete odds.

With the airline's help she made it through the San Diego airport with little trouble. A young sailor with a Southern accent and a shy smile met her in the baggage claim. He had a picture of her and an e-mail from Ford introducing Dawson as her driver. He took control of the luggage, and they were soon on the road to Paradise Pines and the memorial service.

Flying in, the plane had seemed to dodge skyscrapers. Now pulling out of the parking lot she saw those buildings across a harbor view framed by palm trees and a bright blue sky.

The third week of November in San Diego looked, and at seventy-eight degrees, felt a lot different than Scobey, Montana.

"Thirty minutes before the service starts." Rachel checked her watch, pulled it off to reset the time. "Mr. Dawson, how long before we get to Paradise Pines?"

He shot her a grin. "Ma'am, no need for the Mr. It's just Dawson."

"Okay. Please call me Rachel. Do you think we'll make the service on time?"

"We're sure going to try. It's early enough we'll miss traffic, and the church is in Alpine, which is about twelve miles this side of Paradise Pines. You just sit back and relax. I'll have you there in a jiffy."

"Thank you, Dawson. Do you have a cell phone so I can check in with Ford?"

"You don't have a cell?" He sounded shocked.

"No." Not much need for one in Scobey. Heck she rarely used her house phone. "May I borrow yours?"

"Sure, but when I tried Mustang twenty minutes ago to tell him your plane was on time, I got an out of service message. It can be sketchy close to the mountains."

Rachel received the same message. Disappointed, she returned the phone to Dawson.

Once on the road both babies fell asleep. Rachel used the time to freshen her makeup and hair. Dabbing perspiration from her temple, she realized her plan to hide the worst of the wrinkles in her dress under a fitted sweater jacket were out the window.

"Y'all want the air on?" Dawson pressed a few buttons on the console, and blessed cool air flowed from the vents.

"Thanks, I'm overdressed for this heat. It was ten

degrees when I left Montana this morning. It sure is beautiful here."

Forty minutes after leaving the airport, they pulled to a stop in front of Queen of Angels church in Alpine.

"Here ya'll go. You want help with the little ones?"

"Please." Rachel climbed from the SUV and removed Jolie from her seat. Still sleepy, she laid her head on Rachel's shoulder and whined quietly.

"Shh, baby. It's okay." Rachel soothed Jolie while Dawson came around the car with Cody. When he saw her, Cody held his arms out to Rachel. She quickly distracted him with a teething ring.

Tears stung the back of her throat as she approached the church doors. Sadness welled up inside her. Focused on the logistics of the trip, the purpose had receded to the back of her mind. Now it rushed forward intensified by her disappointment in being too late to sit with Ford.

She'd so wanted to get here in time for the twins to be with Ford. For the four of them to be together to support each other in this time of sorrow.

It touched her to see the small church almost filled to capacity. Quaint colored light filtered down on the mourners from beautiful stained-glass windows.

Ford sat on the aisle in the front row. Rachel longed to go to him, but the service had begun. Not wanting to disturb the ceremony, she directed Dawson into the last row of chairs across the aisle from Ford. At least she could take comfort in seeing him and knowing he was near.

A lot cranky and a whole lot less impressed by the proceedings, Cody immediately protested with an annoyed wail.

Ford knew Cody's cry. He swung around, and across the expanse of the small church, he met Rachel's aqua-blue gaze.

Immediately something in him eased. She was here. Finally. It felt as if a lifetime had passed since he'd last seen her.

And here, mourning the loss of his friend, reliving his part in the untimely deaths of these young, vital loved ones, he needed her by his side.

Nobody understood like Rachel. Nobody was as close to the departed as they were, except the twins. And today more than ever he and Rachel stood for the orphaned siblings.

Uncaring of the assemblage, he rose and went to her, watching as Cody, not content to stay with Dawson, climbed into Rachel's lap so she held both twins.

He stopped in front of her. Jolie looked up, saw him and practically leaped into his arms. Rachel rose with a struggling Cody in her arms. Holding Jolie against his heart, Ford drew the other two into his embrace. For a moment he closed his eyes and rested his forehead against Rachel's, absorbing the peace of her presence, the sheer rightness of them being together again.

This, the four of them standing as a family, was the biggest honor they could bestow on Tony and Crystal's memories.

When the quiet of the church registered, Ford looked up to realize the priest had paused out of respect for them. Taking Rachel's hand, he led her to the front row where his family had shifted to make a seat for her.

"This is my grandmother." He whispered the introduction of the petite, gray-haired woman with alert blue eyes.

"My dear." Gram reached for Rachel's hand, squeezed and held on. "I'm so glad you made it."

Ford held Cody in one arm and placed his other around Rachel's shoulders. She held Jolie on her lap. With his family linked in love and support, he nodded to the priest to continue.

A reception at the Sullivan estate in Paradise Pines followed the service. Many of the mourners, plus a few who couldn't attend the service flowed over to Gram's place. A soft blue color with white gingerbread trim, the large Victorian manor sat on a couple of acres of lush green grass and flowering gardens.

A crush of people filled the living room, parlor and kitchen. Rachel quickly lost track of names and faces. She made an effort to note Ford's brothers, a chore made easier by the resemblance between them. She'd met and liked his sister-in-law, Samantha, a green-eyed blonde, who Rachel learned was a school nurse.

The twins were swept away, oohed and aahed over and pretty much spoiled by everyone.

A self-proclaimed loner, Rachel felt a little out of her element and a lot overwhelmed. If not for the twins, she'd have found a quiet corner to escape to. She felt a tug on her hand and turned to find Ford.

"Come, walk with me." He drew her toward the kitchen and the back door. "Samantha has agreed to watch the twins for a while."

"Oh—" she hung back at that news "—I can't let her do that. She has her own boys to watch. It's too much."

"Look around you." He swept a hand out to indicate the crush of people in the kitchen and beyond to the parlor. "She has plenty of help."

Seeing the babies bouncing on the knees of their uncles, she conceded he was right. The twins were in good hands. With them taken care of, the thought of spending time with Ford held great appeal.

"Okay, for a little while."

He grinned and led her outside. "The last time you said that, you slept in my arms."

"Oh snap." Laughing, she chided him. "That was your fault. You were supposed to wake me." Better to make light than to dwell on the peace and rightness she had felt being in his arms.

She'd found she had little impartiality when it came to him.

"Now you tell me." Stopping in the middle of a garden pathway, he wrapped an arm around her waist and pulled her close. "Let me warn you right now, if you're leaving it up to me to watch out for your virtue, there's an old adage that covers this situation."

"Oh?" Breathless at his nearness, at the intensity in his eyes, she was reminded of his dangerous edge. His sexy, seductive, uncompromising appeal. "What's that?"

"All is fair in love and war." Dipping his head, he claimed her lips in an urgent melding of their mouths.

Unlike the slow and dreamy kiss he'd stolen on her porch before leaving Montana, this kiss demanded a response. She answered by rising onto her toes and opening to his sensual assault.

He angled his head, cupped her neck in a sure hand and took the caress deeper. The heat of his passion, the desperation of his touch showed her how much he'd missed her.

She savored the moment as she conveyed her own fierce loneliness.

When he stepped back, she blinked up at him slightly disoriented. His blue eyes were dilated and a red flush stained his earlobes. He glanced behind him, and she realized they still stood in the middle of the garden in full view of the house.

"This way." He led her past the garden and across a green lawn to a small cottage tucked into the back corner of the estate.

"What's this place?" she asked as he foraged for a key in the planter beside the door.

"Guest house." He opened the door and drew her inside. Overstuffed furniture and neutral colors offset with splashes of deep wine gave the room a comfortable feel. "We can talk in here."

Despite his predatory stance and the heat radiating from him, for all his body's readiness to finish what they'd started in the yard, he made no move toward her. Out of respect, she knew, for her. Because she'd made it clear how insane a physical relationship would be in their situation.

Right, sheer lunacy, she thought, as she advanced on him. Just call her crazy.

"Talk?" she asked as he watched her warily. "I think I'm ready to do more than talk."

"It's not that simple between us." He caught her hand when she would have touched him. Holding their clasped hands to his heart, he fought for clarity. "Are you sure this is what you want?"

"Yes." She turned her hand to press against his heavy pounding heart. "I feel alive when you touch me. I feel connected like I never have before." She pushed him toward the couch conveniently located behind him. "I need to feel alive today."

Six feet two inches of hard muscle and bone-deep honor, he didn't budge an inch. "All the more reason I shouldn't take advantage of you."

His resistance should have brought Rachel to her senses. After all, she'd been the one to fight against the attraction between them from the beginning. Except she hadn't lied. Sitting through the memorial service had opened a raw emptiness in her.

Her parents were gone. Her younger sister was gone. Yes, she'd walked away from them in her youth. She'd had her reasons, and she wouldn't really change her decision if she had it to do again. But she'd always known they were there. That she had family out there somewhere. Now she was alone, except for two young babies.

Her sister's children. Crystal had been young but she'd taken chances. She'd lived, she'd loved, she'd created life.

Today Rachel wanted to take chances, she wanted to

live, and she wanted to make love with Ford. If that meant seducing him, she was up to the challenge.

And she promised herself, no regrets.

"You won't be taking advantage of me," she assured him as she slipped behind him where he couldn't hold her off with his superior strength. Twining her arms around his waist she leaned into him, her breasts flat against his back, her cheek between his shoulder blades. "I intend to take advantage of you."

He laughed and she smiled as she felt the rumble vibrate through his body. She wanted this man, this body, this moment more than she'd ever longed for anyone else in her life.

"Am I going to have to get rough with you?" She let her hands wander, enjoyed touching him, thrilled at the tactile contrast between soft silk and hard muscles. He caught her hands when they reached his belt buckle.

He turned around, caught her face in his hands and kissed her with burning urgency.

"Rough can be fun," he whispered against her open mouth, "but it's not necessary. As long as you're sure."

Satisfaction and anticipation ignited her blood. Melting against him, she met his mouth, sank into the kiss. She felt more than alive in his arms, she felt energized, vitalized.

"Ford, we said goodbye to Crystal and Tony today. If life were fair at all, they would have lived to see the twins' first steps, to walk them to kindergarten, to teach them to drive. Tony would have escorted Jolie down the aisle and coached Cody on the finer points of throwing a football.

"But life isn't even close to fair. It's a kick in the

teeth. So instead of Tony and Crystal, the twins are stuck with us. I love the twins. I can't even remember what life was like without them, but I'd give them up quick as a heartbeat if it would bring my sister back."

"Shh." Ford pressed a finger to her lips, followed the gesture with a soft kiss. "Don't go there. It's useless speculation, and you're the one who kicked my butt about second-guessing fate."

"I know. I'm sorry." She wiped away a tear she'd sworn to keep locked away and almost lost it when he captured her finger to absorb the tear with his kiss. She cleared her throat. "I didn't mean to get maudlin. My point is I'm beyond sure. I want to be with you. More, I need the comfort and escape I'll find in your arms."

To show him just how certain, her fingers went to the buttons of her new black dress. She'd been looking for a reason to get out of the dress since she landed in San Diego. No better reason than this.

"Make me forget that they're gone, Ford. Let me remind you why it's good to be alive."

She released the third button, revealing the first rise of cleavage before Ford took over.

"Dynamite, you did that the minute you opened your door in Scobey." He made short work of the rest of the buttons. "Lucky for both of us, I'm a SEAL. The Boy Scouts have nothing on us for being prepared."

He was talking about birth control, telling her he had it covered. His assurance warmed her. She'd been running on emotion, hadn't thought that far ahead. Thank goodness his cool head ruled.

The heat of his breath caressed the curve of her neck

as the dress fell off her shoulders and to the floor, leaving her in nothing but a black bra and thong.

The sexy lingerie was another new purchase. Obviously her subconscious at work.

His eyes cherished her before his mouth began the same downward journey. Time slowed and lengthened while desire bloomed.

Suddenly her clothes were gone and he lowered her to the downy softness of a bed. Sensation replaced all else as he took her to heights she'd never known before. Precious, he made her feel so precious, using his mouth, fingers, and body to worship every inch of her.

She reciprocated touch for touch, kiss for kiss, stroke for stroke, thrilling when she drew groans of satisfaction from him. Wrapping her arms around him, she clung on tightly and followed him to the explosive realm of completion.

Ford sighed, contentment flowing through him along with the soft peach scent of Rachel's shampoo. He tightened his arm around her and buried his nose in her hair.

She smelled so good, felt so good. He'd known they'd be volatile in bed, but he'd been wrong. Oh, there'd been explosive chemistry between them, bursting gratification. But what they'd just shared went beyond the physical.

He cared about her and that infused the act with a special sense of fulfillment. She'd talked about being connected. He now knew what she'd meant. He couldn't remember the last time he'd felt so close to another human being.

She slipped past his defenses with her sassy attitude and fragile vulnerability. Yet he hadn't realized how much he missed her until she hadn't made it to the church before the start of the memorial service.

Even surrounded by family and friends, he'd felt as if he were all alone. Then she arrived and seeing her and the twins had grounded him, allowed him to make it through the emotional ceremony.

Now more than ever he wanted her to move to San Diego. With her here he wouldn't worry about Cody and Jolie. He'd have felt good about leaving them with his family, but as she'd pointed out, Rachel was their family. The twins wouldn't have to earn her love. She gave it unconditionally.

And he liked the thought of her being here when he came home between assignments. It was the best of both worlds.

This time Rachel slid away from a sleeping Ford. She barely breathed until she'd retrieved her clothes and ducked into the bathroom.

No regrets. That's what she promised herself. She'd taken a chance and received glorious results. Being with Ford exceeded all her fantasies. And revealed a scary new facet to their relationship.

She loved him.

She loved his honor, his gentleness, his generosity. She loved that he knew the sound of Cody's cry, that he had shed tears at the loss of his friend, that he loved and respected his grandmother. She loved his tough as nails exterior and soft as marshmallow interior. Through him she'd discovered that duty and responsibility weren't always used to squash down those in your care, but sometimes meant dealing with compromise and hard decisions.

All these soft feelings scared her to death. Because she'd be a fool to mistake his passion for anything more than casual affection. She knew the sad truth of unrequited love too well to risk rejection when the twins' future hung in the balance.

No doubt about it, her best course of action was to pretend this little incident never happened. She slipped out of the bathroom and made it all the way to the front door, when Ford spoke behind her.

"Don't go."

Her hand tightened on the doorknob. Two seconds more and she'd have been on the other side of the door.

"I don't just mean now. I mean for good." She felt his heat as he came to stand behind her. Snuggling close to her back, he ran his hand down her arm to link his fingers with hers. "Please stay."

The words seemed to echo in the stillness. His request brought her dilemma front and center.

Electing to remain turned away in case any of her newly acknowledged emotions showed on her face, she responded, "I promised I'd think about moving. I know it's the perfect solution to the custody issue, but it's a big decision. I need time."

"I don't mean just move to San Diego." He gently turned her to face him, traced the curve of her cheek with a knuckle. "I mean stay with me, move in with me."

Stay with Ford? The thought both terrified and exhilarated Rachel. Yes, she loved him and she longed to be with him, but her life was in Montana, what she had to offer the twins was in Montana. She could write anywhere, but her home was in Montana.

Dare she give up the life she'd made, which until a month ago was all she'd had to define herself?

"I'm so glad you made it in time for the service." The huskiness in his voice revealed emotions close to the surface. "I was lost until you got there."

"Oh, Ford." His unexpected vulnerability tore her apart.

"It was important to me that you and the twins were there because we've become a family." He kissed her ear, her neck, the corner of her mouth. "Let's make a home together, you, me and the twins. We can move in here until we find a bigger place."

She looked into his eyes, gauged his expression. She saw earnestness along with affection, determination, and desire in his sapphire gaze.

But love? Could what he felt for her grow into something stronger?

She'd taken a huge chance by making love with him, and suffered no regrets. Could she take it one step further?

"It's too complicated. We have to think of the future."

His mouth teased hers. "We won't let it get complicated. We'll take it one day at a time. As long as we're honest with each other and put the twins first, we keep it simple."

Her mind urged caution, but her heart wanted to believe. She threaded her fingers through his silky, dark hair and pulled him down for a kiss.

Against his mouth, she whispered. "I'll stay."

CHAPTER ELEVEN

RACHEL followed Ford into the kitchen of the main house. Only the family remained. His brothers sat around the huge butcher-block table while Gram and Samantha watched over the four children from armchairs near the fireplace in what used to be the parlor. Ford's cousin Mattie stood at the counter making a new pot of coffee.

Laughter and chatter filled the room, happy sounds compared to the somber gathering they'd left behind earlier. The rich scent of brewing coffee added to the homey feel of the room.

"I'll take a cup of that." Ford opened a cupboard and took down a mug. He looked at Rachel and at her nod grabbed a second mug. While he waited for the coffee to finish, he faced the room.

"I have an announcement. Rachel has decided to move to California. We're going to get a place and raise the twins together."

Silence greeted his statement. For five full seconds. Then pandemonium broke out. Everyone started talking at once, well wishes overlapped questions of concern, and advice on buying versus renting.

Unused to such chaos Rachel just let it wash over and around her until Gram came forward and squeezed Rachel's hands.

"My dear, welcome." Gram kissed Rachel's cheek.

Rachel gave her a hug. "Thank you, Mrs. Sullivan. I also want to tell you how much I appreciate all you, and your family, did in arranging the memorial service today."

"Call me Gram." The older woman waved away the formalities. "I was happy to help honor Tony and Crystal. Tony was dear to me. Crystal, I only met a couple of times, but she was full of life, and she loved those babies. Such a loss, for them, for you, for the world."

The simple sympathy caught Rachel unawares. Tears swelled up and overflowed. She'd done so well at maintaining her cool through the day, keeping her tears to the service. But then it all suddenly caught up with her. So much had happened, not least of all discovering her love for Ford, that Gram's words of comfort tipped Rachel over the edge.

"It's okay, you go ahead and cry." Gram pulled Rachel into her arms and rubbed her back soothingly.

Instantly Ford appeared at their sides, but Gram shooed him away. "I've got her, she just needs a little cry is all. Why don't you put together a plate of food to heat when she's ready? I noticed she didn't eat much earlier."

Ford kissed her hair and whispered, "Take your time. I'm here if you need me." Then went off to do as directed.

So gentle, so sweet. Rachel just sobbed harder.

Gram led her to a couch in the quiet of the living room. "I've got you," Gram said, holding Rachel in her arms. "Go ahead and cry."

Unable to resist the comfort of a motherly embrace, something she'd known so little of in her life, Rachel clung to Gram and let the tears flow.

"I like it." Rachel glanced around the medium-size kitchen of the prospective rental in Alpine. She'd insisted on renting at this point. Everything was moving so fast, falling so easily into place, she didn't completely trust it.

She and Ford had looked at houses with larger kitchens, but she liked the openness of this one. It reminded her of the setup of her home in Montana. No island, but a breakfast bar separated the kitchen from the family room. Like Gram's parlor, the family room had a fireplace.

Cautiously optimistic, Rachel could see the four of them spending lots of happy moments in these two rooms.

"I like it, too." Ford opened a pantry door, nodded and closed it again. "Only three bedrooms, but that's enough until the twins get older. The master suite is huge, great walk-in shower."

"We don't really need three bedrooms. We could find a two bedroom for less."

Shaking his head, Ford came to her, curved his arm around her waist and pulled her close. "We're only going to have two bedrooms and an office. I want you to have your own space to write."

"Ford—"

"Shh." He stopped her with a kiss. "I know the rent seems high compared to Scobey, but money is not a problem. We can afford any place we want."

Money wasn't a problem for him. He'd explained he held an interest in the family jewelry store, Sullivans' Jewels. Which apparently did quite well. She found the family's net worth somewhat intimidating.

She had decent savings, by Montana standards, but she couldn't help thinking she'd have been in real trouble if she'd had to fight Ford for custody.

"Money does matter." She wouldn't be a slouch in this relationship. Her independence had been too important to her for too long for her to change now. "I want to pay my share."

"You will." He promised, sweeping his mouth across hers. "You already have with all you bought for the babies. And I promise to let you pay for the utilities."

Her tension eased at his assurances and the look of understanding in his eyes.

"Okay, then." She leaned against him and looked around the kitchen one more time. "So, shall we put in an application for this place?"

"Yeah. We can take it with us to fill out tonight, and you can drop it off tomorrow."

He'd gone back to work the Monday after the memorial service. And she missed him so much. Gram, Samantha and Mattie kept her company and helped with the twins so Rachel got plenty of time to write. Yet she still lived for the end of the day when he returned home to her arms.

"Sounds like a plan." She agreed. "The ad said available for immediate occupancy. Do you think we'll be able to move in over the long weekend?"

"That's the beauty of city life, babe." He tucked a stray

lock of hair behind her ear. "Except for Thanksgiving the rest of the weekend is business as usual."

"Great, then we can move this weekend." She made to move away, but Ford held her in place.

"About this weekend. There's something I have to tell you."

Her heart started to pound, her mouth went dry, and dread grew heavy in her gut. She knew. By the seriousness of his expression and the leeriness shadowing the blue in his eyes.

"You're leaving on assignment."

"Yeah." He rubbed his forehead. "We're already on call. When we go in tomorrow we'll go into lockdown for planning and prep. I don't know when I'll see you again."

Wow, here it was.

Fear for him rose up in a tidal wave. She wanted to scream out a protest, to say no he couldn't go. He couldn't leave her and the twins. But she'd known what she'd been signing up for when she'd agreed to stay, to be a part of his life.

He supported her independence; she owed him the same respect, the freedom to be who he was. It's the advice she'd given Crystal; Rachel would be a fool not to take it herself.

Of course, that didn't stop the emotions from roiling through her. But she refused to give into the worry and dread, instead she chose to make the most of the time she had before he left tomorrow morning.

"Let's go home." Lifting onto her toes, she kissed the frown from his mouth. "Do you think Alex and Samantha would baby-sit? I want you to myself tonight."

* * *

In the predawn light Ford stood quietly next to the bed. Already packed, his duffle waited by the front door.

Time to say goodbye.

He didn't want to do it. Which set up all kinds of conflicting emotions inside him, satisfaction at being able to rejoin his SEAL team but reluctance at leaving Rachel. And regret that he'd miss a moment of the twins' development—he just knew Cody would walk any day now.

Ford stood gazing down at Rachel. Her short blond hair curled softly around her face while her long dark lashes fanned across her creamy skin. She looked like an angel tucked beneath the sheets. The last of the moonlight slanted a dim glow over an alabaster shoulder.

He grinned. A naked angel.

She'd slept little if at all during the night. His smile lingered at the corner of his mouth. They'd spent hours making love, from hard and fast, to sweet and sassy, to heart wrenchingly slow.

Only when they were both exhausted did he wrap her in his arms to sleep. Even with all the expended energy he knew she'd slept little. She'd pretended to sleep, as she was doing now.

To save them from the moment of goodbye.

He'd done that in the past, slipped out after a sensuous farewell. Because it was easier for everyone that way. More anonymous, less intense, especially when the emotions didn't run that deep.

Rachel deserved better than a hit-and-run. Standing over her, with death a true possibility on the other side of the door, saying goodbye rated as the hardest thing he'd ever done.

For that reason, it had to be face-to-face, eye-to-eye.

As if her thoughts brought her to the same conclusion at the same time, her stunning aqua eyes opened. All the anxiety and uncertainty she felt showed in her gleaming gaze.

"Hey," she said softly, sitting up so the sheet pulled tight across her breasts.

"Hey." Ford sat down next to her. Needing to touch, he cupped the back of her neck and ran his thumb over the silkiness of her cheek.

Because the words wouldn't come, he bent and put his feelings in a kiss, all his adoration, passion and torment. Her response equaled his in emotional impact.

When it reached the point where he needed to climb into bed or pull back, he lifted his head. "Promise me you'll let my family help you."

That earned him a wan smile. "I promise."

Knowing the time had come, he stood. He held out a hand. "Walk me out?"

She slipped out of bed, wrapped the sheet around herself and laced her fingers through his. He led her to the front door where his duffle waited.

Pulling her into his arms, he pressed his nose into her mussed curls. "Kiss the twins for me."

"I will." She looked up, framed his face in trembling hands. "Wild Mustang, come back to me."

I will, the words were on the tip of his tongue, but they both knew it was a promise he couldn't make. Instead he gave her one last, hard kiss and stepped out the door.

* * *

"Oh my goodness, Cody is walking," Samantha called out, drawing everyone's attention to where she and Rachel were sitting on the floor in front of the parlor fireplace.

Gathered together for Thanksgiving Day. Rachel sat among Ford's family in Gram's house and clapped along with the others as Cody wobbled from her hold to Samantha's. Her pride in Cody's accomplishment only suffered from Ford's absence. She knew he'd regret missing this special moment.

"Hey, little buddy, walk to Uncle Cole."

The Sullivans were a rowdy crowd, boisterous and giving. They'd welcomed her and the twins into their midst with warmth and generosity. The twins thrived in the loving environment, which showed in Cody's zigzag journey around the room as he walked from uncle to aunt to uncle.

Rachel did her best to fit in, but too many years on her own gave her a reticence that couldn't be shrugged aside so easily. Ford's brothers, bless them, gave her both space and casual affection.

Gram, Samantha and Ford's cousin Mattie drew her in and made her one of the crowd. No distance allowed here. Rachel accepted their good-hearted advice and interference with surprising tolerance.

Leaving the twins in the capable hands of the family, Rachel slipped out to the front porch. Last week's heat had given way to a cold front, and the nip in the air made her wish she'd grabbed her sweater.

In moments like this one she missed Ford all the more, not just for her sake but for his as well. His excitement when Jolie had walked had matched Rachel's.

She knew he'd be disappointed to miss this milestone in Cody's life.

The door opened behind her and Ford's oldest brother Alex stepped out on the porch. Tall, dark and broad, with the Sullivan blue eyes, the resemblance between him and Ford was striking. But there were differences, too. Alex carried more weight and showed the beginnings of gray in his hair and he lacked Ford's dangerous edge.

"I guess you're missing Ford about now." Alex came to stand beside her.

"Yeah." She leaned her hip against the railing and faced him. "And I guess you've come out to give me the third degree."

He shrugged and propped a shoulder against a post. "What makes you think that?"

"I know animals. This is your pack. You need to check out the new member."

"I won't apologize for protecting my family." Totally confident, neither his stance nor his expression changed.

"I don't expect you to," she assured him, though she didn't back down. "Now I'm responsible for the twins, I have a whole new respect for what a parent will do to protect their family."

"And how far will you go for the twins, Rachel?"

A half smile tugged at the corner of her mouth. "Somehow I don't think you're referring to the distance between Montana and San Diego."

"Once Ford sets his mind to something, it takes dynamite to change his course. He left here intending to bring the twins back, to raise them within the family. And that's exactly what he did. But you, you're a surprise."

She lifted a brow. "And you want to know if I'm taking advantage of him?"

"You've known my brother for little more than a month, yet you're living with him, raising children together. That's damn fast work."

"Do you think it would be so easy to make Ford do something he didn't want to do?"

He rolled his eyes. "You're a beautiful woman, what's not to want. You should know Ford isn't ready to settle down. For a commitment. He's not called Mustang for nothing."

"I don't think you give him enough credit, which is a shame, because I know your opinion matters to him." She crossed her arms over her chest. "Ford is the most generous, caring man I know."

Alex cocked a dark brow. "He's my brother, I think I know him better than you."

"You should, but you don't. You ought to know by now he doesn't like to be told what to do. The two most important things in his life are the SEALs and his family. He's committed to both. Having to choose between them is tearing him apart. A little support from you would be helpful, and I'm not talking about giving advice. I'm talking about supporting whatever decision he makes regardless of whether you approve or not."

By Alex's stark expression she saw she'd hit a nerve, had given him something to think about. Rachel drew in a deep breath, breathed out. She needed to compose herself. Being with Ford meant being a part of his family.

"It's hard as hell," she said more calmly. "But that's what I'm offering him, because it's what I'd want from him, and I respect him too much to force my fears on him." She forced a smile. "It may reassure you to know no promises have been made between us. None are necessary."

Pensive, Alex stuffed his hands in his pockets. He frowned as he focused on her.

"Is that fair to you?" he asked.

Now she smiled for real. "You can't help yourself, can you? You have to take care of everyone." She moved to him, watched the wariness come into his eyes, but all she did was give him a kiss on the cheek. "You're sweet, but this is where Ford and I are right now. As you said, we've only known each other for a month. We'll work it out."

"And that's good enough for you?"

"Oh, yeah. Mustangs are famous for being wild and free, but they make great domestic animals if you don't break their spirit." And because she'd reached the limit on what she felt comfortable revealing to him, she turned to the house. At the door she stopped and glanced back at him. "Alex?"

He looked over his shoulder at her, one dark brow lifted in query.

"Ford has a nickname for me, do you know what it is?"

Alex shook his head. "What?"

"Dynamite." With a wink and a grin, she stepped into the house.

Rachel spent Friday and Saturday packing and shopping for furniture. Before he left, Ford had arranged for the baby furniture at her place in Montana to be packed up and shipped to Alpine. The rest of the stuff could wait until she had time to make a trip.

In the meantime Samantha volunteered to help so they left the children in the care of Sami's regular baby-sitter and set out to put a home together.

The first course of action was to inventory Ford's condo in downtown San Diego to see what they wanted to take and what they'd need to buy new.

"I like this dining room set, but I think I prefer using the living room furniture from the cottage to this black leather." Rachel stood hands on her hips surveying the setup.

"I agree and Gram said you were welcome to use whatever you need." Sami swept a long length of blond hair behind her ear. "What's Ford going to do with this place?"

"He talked about renting it. I told him we could stay here, but he wanted the twins and me to be closer to the family when he was gone." Rachel walked down the hall into the master bedroom. "Oh, this is beautiful."

A lovely king-size mahogany framed bed dominated the room. Matching bedside tables and a large bureau completed the set. The comforter was a scrumptious red satin with oriental motifs.

Rachel loved it, but only one thing came to mind when she looked at it. She met Sami's gaze.

"New bedroom set," they both said at the same time.

CHAPTER TWELVE

BY SHEER force of will and instincts honed by years of experience, Ford made it through the assignment without getting anyone killed. Himself included.

Rachel invaded his mind every minute of every day. And the twins, he couldn't help wondering whether they were all safe and sound.

While the team worked to rescue a politician's daughter from a hostage situation, he worried about his little corner of the world.

Lord, he thought, he'd missed Rachel in the week between leaving Montana and her arrival in San Diego. The whole world had seemed dimmer that week.

He'd known before she'd even got to San Diego, he wouldn't be letting her leave. He'd been prepared for a fight, and to do whatever it took to win.

Instead she'd surprised him with a soft and giving acceptance he knew had cost her hugely in trust and independence. The next week he'd literally and figuratively lived in Paradise.

Everything fell into place. He went back to work. Gram helped Rachel with the twins during the day so she had time for her writing. And at night they'd been together as a family until they closed the bedroom door and he had Rachel all to himself.

"Hey man, how you doing?" Hoss, massive, dark skinned, bald headed, and a straight shooter on and off assignment sat down next to Ford.

"Not good." Ford bent his head, scrubbed at his eyes with the heels of his hands. "I was a mess out there."

"You held it together."

"Barely. And that kind of distraction gets people killed." A SEAL always knew danger was an inherent part of any assignment, but they put that out of their mind and did the job.

In the past Ford had embraced the impartiality needed to accomplish the task. This time he couldn't forget he had people at home counting on his safe return. People he longed to see again, to hold in his arms, to cherish.

"So what *are* you going to do?" Hoss asked.

Ford summoned a grin he didn't feel. "I called ahead, got a meeting with the CO to explore my options."

"You know Intelligence would scoop you up in a heartbeat."

Ford rubbed a weary hand over the tight muscles of his neck. "Yeah. Man, you remember BUDS training?"

"Hell, yeah. You thinking of training? Those instructors are tough bastards." Hoss eyed Ford thoughtfully, nodded. "You'd be great."

"You think? Rachel suggested it. The idea is growing on me."

"Woman knows her man." Hoss held up his hand and they bumped knuckles. "Good luck, Mustang."

When he reached the base, Ford went straight to the commander's office. He knocked, and then stepped inside at his CO's wave.

Ford saluted. "Sir. I'm here to request a transfer."

With all the excitement of the move and ending the day in a new house, the twins were over excited and refused to settle down on Sunday night. Rachel glanced at her watch. After nine. She'd hoped to get some unpacking done, instead she threw pillows down on the living room carpet and let the kids loose.

Restrained most of the day both of them immediately climbed up to practice their new favorite thing, walking.

"You two are tired, so be careful." Rachel perched on the edge of the sofa ready to spring into action if needed.

Jolie grinned and walked straight to Rachel.

"Hey, beautiful. You're getting good at this aren't you? Cody has some catching up to do doesn't he?"

Hearing his name Cody turned from where he stood by the coffee table and waved his arms. His weight shifted and he started to fall.

"No." Rachel saw it happening, saw it and couldn't stop it. She jumped up but couldn't reach Cody before he fell hard against the edge of the hardwood table. He twisted trying to compensate, but instead of saving himself he hit the table hard splitting his forehead open.

Cody screamed.

Blood spurted everywhere.

Jolie began to cry.

"Oh God. Oh God." Heart in her throat Rachel scooped Cody up in one arm and Jolie in the other and rushed to the bathroom. She put Jolie in the dry tub and took Cody to the sink.

"It's okay, baby, it's okay." God she prayed it was okay.

She tried to wash the wound but the gash was deep and wouldn't stop bleeding. Her mind spun as she considered what to do. She tore a new pillowcase into strips and wrapped a makeshift bandage around his head.

The hospital, she needed to get Cody to the hospital.

Grabbing a baby in each arm she carried them both to the crib, and then went to the kitchen to call Alex and Samantha. They'd left an hour ago. She hated to drag them back, but she didn't know where the hospital was, and if they could watch Jolie…

"Shoot." No answer. And no time to keep trying. She tried Cole's number, but again received no reply. She elected not to leave messages because they'd only worry and there'd be no way for them to reach her.

Damn. First thing tomorrow morning she was getting a cell phone.

It was after two when Ford reached home. He'd decided to stop off in Alpine in case Rachel had managed to arrange the move over the long weekend as she'd wanted to do. And sure enough lights blazed from several rooms.

He didn't have a key yet so he knocked. Then knocked louder. No answer. Utilizing skills he usually restricted to national security, he unlocked the door and stepped inside.

He immediately spotted the blood in the hall, in the living room. Adrenaline shot through his system.

"Rachel," he called out, following the blood trail down the hall. His stomach flipped when he spied the mess in the bathroom. "Rachel!"

He pulled out his phone, called Gram. She hadn't heard from Rachel since early evening. Next he tried Alex and Sami. Alex reported they'd left Rachel and the twins around eight-thirty. Everyone had been fine. They had a missed call from her a little after nine, but she hadn't left a message.

"Grossmont is the nearest hospital," Alex reasoned.

"I'm on my way." Ford was already climbing into his Jeep.

"I'll call and see if I can learn anything. Don't worry, Ford, we'll find them. Was Rachel's SUV in the driveway?"

"No." Ford cursed. "And I didn't stop to check the garage."

"It was in the driveway when we left, that means Rachel was able to drive them wherever they went. That's something at least."

"Yeah." Ford disconnected. His stomach churned. Bloody scenarios raced through his head. The fact that Rachel had been able to drive offered little consolation. He just wanted to find them all safe.

Then he'd talk to Rachel about taking off without letting anyone know where she was going or what had happened.

He made the twenty-mile drive to Grossmont Hospital in twelve minutes. He stormed up to the nurse's station. "I'm looking for Rachel Adams. Are they here?"

"Ford?" The voice came from behind him. "Ford!"

He turned in time to catch Rachel as she launched herself into his arms. "I'm so glad you're here."

"Rachel." He breathed her name, more a prayer of thanksgiving than a greeting. He squeezed her to him, buried his face in her hair. "Tell me you're all right."

Rachel wrapped her arms around Ford and held on tight. For the first time in hours her world felt right. Tears held at bay for so long broke free. She clung to Ford, wanting nothing more than to burrow into the safety of his arms.

"Rachel!" He pushed her away, held her at arm's length. Concern bleached his features of color. "Talk to me. What happened?"

Swiping tears from her face she struggled for composure. "Cody—" She hiccupped and a fresh wave of tears flowed as she remembered her panic and fear when he hurt himself.

"What about Cody?" Ford walked around her to get to the twins in their double stroller. Both babies slept. Cody sported a white bandage across the length of his forehead. "My God." Ford crouched down by the boy. "Tell me what happened."

"He fell." Her breath hitched; again she brushed the wetness from her cheeks. "It was after everyone left. Th-they, the twins wouldn't settle down so I l-let them out to walk around."

"Cody is walking?".

She nodded, breathed deep. "On Thanksgiving. He fell tonight, hit his head on the coffee table. It took six stitches to close the gash."

"Good God." Ford shot to his feet and rolled the

stroller outside. He stopped and confronted her. "Alex said you were moving all weekend, that they didn't leave until after eight. You all had to be exhausted. How could you be so careless?"

Stunned Rachel backed up a step. She blinked away the last of the tears. "What?"

Ford's cell phone rang. He took it out, flipped it open. "Hi, Alex. Thanks, I found them. Cody fell and cut his head. We're taking him home now." He listened. "Yeah, she's fine. Hey can I give you a call tomorrow? Thanks."

He flipped the phone closed, pocketed it. "Let's go. I'll drive. We can leave my Jeep here and pick it up tomorrow." He held out his hand. "Give me your keys."

Chilled inside and out by his cold and accusatory attitude, she led the way to her SUV, helped put the children in their seats, stored the stroller in the back, but when it came to climbing in next to him the tension broke her.

"I don't think so." She crossed her arms under her breasts. "Not until you explain your accusation."

He stalked around the vehicle to confront her. "You're the one that needs to explain a few things." He paced away, then back, his movements jerky, out of control.

"Do you know what it was like to walk into the house tonight and find blood everywhere? To call my brother and find out you couldn't be bothered to leave a message about what happened or to say where you were?" He raked both hands through his hair, shook his head. "On top of that selfishness I find out this could all have been avoided if you'd used a little common sense."

"Enough," she demanded. Not since he'd first landed

on her doorstep had he been so critical of her. So cold. She'd spent the last hours wishing he were here to help her, to hold her. To make everything all right. How cruel of fate to grant her wish only to deliver this antagonistic stranger.

"I've just spent four hours beating myself up over Cody's accident, but I'll be damned if I'll stand here and take criticism from you when you don't know what you're talking about." She shook with anger, with disappointment, with betrayal.

She spread her arms wide, exhibiting the rust-colored bloodstains on her blue shirt and jeans. "Yeah, there was blood in the house, lots of it, so excuse me if I chose to get Cody to the hospital rather than chase down your family, who'd already spent the weekend helping us move. And no I didn't leave a message because I couldn't wait for them to respond, and I didn't know where I was going so why worry them unnecessarily?"

Beyond weary, she swayed where she stood.

He'd gone still and quiet during her diatribe, now seeing signs of her weakness, he reached for her arm. "Come on, let's go home, we'll talk about this tomorrow."

"I'm not going anywhere with you." She dodged his touch, rounded the hood of the SUV and got behind the wheel. He followed her, but when he reached for the door handle she hit the locks.

"Rachel, open the door." He knocked on the window. A frown drew his dark brows together. He looked tired and drawn. "You're upset. Let me drive."

Tears came back, blurring her vision. She blinked

them away and put the car in gear. She drove away without a backward glance.

Rachel was greeted for the empty streets—it compensated for the fact that her full attention wasn't on the road. On a lonely stretch of Freeway 8 at 2:55 in the morning reality hit her square in the face. Ford only asked her to stay so he could leave. By agreeing to stay she'd only set herself up for a repeat of her childhood, to live where she was valued more for what she did— care for the twins—than for who she was—a strong and independent woman.

A strong and independent woman foolishly in love.

Shame on her for dropping her guard, for believing, even for a moment, something special had developed between her and Ford. Love of the self-sacrificing, unconditional variety didn't exist between men and women.

Giving up her home, setting aside the protection of her loner ways had earned her nothing more than a broken heart.

Disillusioned, angry with him and herself, she realized she couldn't stay in San Diego. When Cody was well enough to travel she'd take the twins and fly back to Montana. With the decision made she went numb, her emotions and subconscious shutting down to protect her from the too familiar sense of loss and betrayal.

Aware of Ford following behind her, she almost didn't go to the house in Alpine, the house she'd taken such joy in preparing for their family, but it took more energy than she possessed to think where else to go.

She parked in the driveway, released Jolie from her seat and carried her to her crib, carefully avoiding any sight of the blood throughout the house. Cleanup could wait until later.

Ford arrived with Cody, gently lowering the baby into his crib. Rachel felt his gaze as she changed Jolie and got the little girl situated. She ignored him, unable to deal with him any further tonight.

She breathed easier when he moved to the door without speaking. She'd be even happier if he'd left the room entirely, but he lingered by the door watching her.

Forcing herself to focus, she went to Cody and woke him as instructed, checking his pupils and level of alertness. Both seemed fine so she changed him and then lifted him and pointed to Ford, because regardless of what was or wasn't between the two of them, she knew he cared about the twins.

"Look who's here," she said.

A grin broke across Cody's face and he held out his little arms.

Ford cradled Cody against his chest and felt something click into place deep inside. Cody and Jolie had pulled on his heartstrings until his heart had grown big enough to embrace them both. He had a lifetime love affair going on here.

Trailing Rachel to the kitchen where she prepared a bottle, Ford knew she was part of the package. More, she was the heart of it.

Boy he'd blown it big time tonight. An overload of adrenaline had caused him to come out blazing when he should have provided a strong, comforting refuge in the face of her ordeal.

Rachel had told him how she'd left home at such a

young age because she'd felt unwelcome within her own family, and what did he do but make her feel an outsider again by putting more importance on informing his family of the emergency than of praising her for her handling of the distressing incident.

"I'm sorry," he said to her back as she stood waiting for the microwave to heat Cody's bottle.

Her shoulders tensed; otherwise she gave no sign of hearing him.

"I'm an idiot. No, that's not strong enough." He crossed the room to stand behind her. "I'm an insensitive ass."

"If you're waiting for an argument from me, you won't get it." The microwave dinged. She made no move to remove the bottle. Or to face Ford.

Not a problem, Cody was already sleeping on Ford's shoulder.

"I've decided to return to Montana." With the declaration, Rachel turned to look him in the eye. "And I'm taking the twins with me."

"No." The hurt and lack of hope in her gaze tore him apart. He'd done that to her.

For a man of action he'd sure been slacking. He'd failed to tell her of his feelings, been afraid to admit his love just as he'd been afraid to give up the excitement of his job. It was time he stepped up. "You can't go. I won't let you leave. I love you."

Rachel frantically shook her head, sidestepped away from Ford, and wrapped her arms around herself.

"You have no say." She completely disregarded his declaration of love as too late, too convenient. "I'll pay for the month's rent. The furnishings can be returned.

You're right, your family is special, the twins are lucky to have them in their lives, but I'm keeping them until you leave the SEALs behind. And you're going to let me because it's the decent thing to do."

Her throat tightened before she finished, a sure sign tears threatened. Refusing to break down in front of him now, she started for the kitchen door.

"Please put Cody in his crib. I have to wake him every hour but first I have to get out of these bloody clothes."

"Rachel, wait—"

"No, just no." She escaped before he tempted her with his easy charm.

In her room she grabbed clean clothes and locked herself in the bathroom where she let the shower wash away the tears. She'd started the day with so much joy, with such anticipation of finally living her dream of love and a family. Hearing Ford announce his love should have been the ultimate high of the day instead of a devastating betrayal of everything good between them.

Unable to stay hidden forever, she dressed and opened the door.

Ford leaned against the doorjamb. He held up a packet of folded papers.

"What's this?"

"Transfer forms. I talked to my CO when we reached base. A master chief instructor at the training facility is retiring next month. I'll be taking his place."

"Why?" She took the papers, opened them to read. "I thought you wanted to finish on your own terms."

"These are my terms." He led her over to the bed, sat down beside her. "I was a mess in the field. I couldn't get you or the twins out of my head. I love you, Rachel. Nothing is more important to me than building a life with you, Jolie and Cody. And maybe a baby of our own someday."

Oh, unfair. Longing and fear battled inside her. "I can't. Tonight—"

"Tonight I overreacted. I was so scared. When I found you all safe I went into an adrenaline crash and I lashed out. But I was wrong. You were smart, and brave, and you made all the right choices."

She shook her head, she wanted to believe but she didn't dare.

"It's no use, you know." He brought her hand to his mouth and kissed her palm. "I know you love me."

That burned her; she snatched her hand away. "You think you know what?"

"You don't fool me. Not once during the argument at the hospital did you throw my job up at me. No reference to missing the twins' first Thanksgiving, to having to handle the move on your own, or to blaming me for not being there when Cody fell. All kill shots. But you didn't make them, why not?"

She looked away from him. "It was already ugly enough."

"Uh-huh, my little piece of dynamite. You never held back when it came to protecting the twins. You could have decimated me, but you didn't." He lifted her chin, forcing her to meet his gaze. "For two reasons. First you love me, and second because of your past. Subconsciously you believe all the nonsense I was spewing. But I was wrong, so wrong."

She swallowed the lump in her throat as she realized she'd fallen into her old familiar role. Drawing in a deep breath, she let the tension go. She refused to give the past power over the future.

"You truly think I was brave?"

"Very brave." He leaned in for a kiss, keeping it slow and gentle. "I'm the SEAL, but you're the one with all the courage. You gave up your home to move here, to be with me, to make a home for the twins. Don't give up on us now."

"If you're transferring to training, you'll be here for the twins. You don't need me to stay."

"I never needed you to stay for the twins. It was always for me."

"Really?"

He pressed her back into the bed. "Oh, yeah."

Rachel looked up into his blue eyes; saw the love shining there for her. "I stayed for you."

"I know." He claimed her mouth, and her love with a passionate sweep of his tongue, deepening the kiss when she wrapped her arms around his neck and lifted into his embrace. "Let's make it permanent."

She pulled back, threaded her fingers through his silky hair. He made her feel so cherished. Yet… "Ford, we didn't make it through our first day in our own home."

"Because I didn't respect what we have. Love is both simple and complicated, easy and hard. Heartache and joy. As long as we stay true to love, as long as we don't give up on each other, we'll make it together. Forget one day at a time, I want forever. Marry me."

Oh God, she wanted to believe him. In truth she'd

changed over the last month. Ford and Cody and Jolie had collectively shattered the barrier she had used to buffer herself from the rest of the world. She was stronger because of the love they'd brought to her life.

Her mind urged her to run, but her heart begged her to stay. Deciding to take a risk on love, she pulled him down for a kiss.

"Yes," she whispered against his mouth. "I'll stay. Forever."

* * * * *

Welcome to cowboy country…

Turn the page for a sneak preview of
TEXAS BABY
by
Kathleen O'Brien
An exciting new title from Harlequin Superromance
for everyone who loves stories about the West.

Harlequin Superromance—
Where life and love weave together
in emotional and unforgettable ways.

CHAPTER ONE

CHASE TRANSFERRED his gaze to the road and identified a foreign spot on the horizon. A car. Almost half a mile away, where the straight, tree-lined drive met the public road. He could tell it was coming too fast, but judging the speed of a vehicle moving straight toward you was tricky.

It wasn't until it was about two hundred yards away that he realized the driver must be drunk…or crazy. Or both.

The guy was going maybe sixty. On a private drive, out here in ranch country, where kids or horses or tractors or stupid chickens might come darting out any minute, that was criminal. Chase straightened from his comfortable slouch and waved his hands.

"Slow down, you fool," he called out. He took the porch steps quickly and began walking fast down the driveway.

The car veered oddly, from one lane to another, then up onto the slight rise of the thick green spring grass. It just barely missed the fence.

"Slow down, damn it!"

He couldn't see the driver, and he didn't recognize this

automobile. It was small and old, and couldn't have cost much even when it was new. It was probably white, but now it needed either a wash or a new paint job or both.

"Damn it, what's wrong with you?"

At the last minute, he had to jump away, because the idiot behind the wheel clearly wasn't going to turn to avoid a collision. He couldn't believe it. The car kept coming, finally slowing a little, but it was too late.

Still going about thirty miles an hour, it slammed into the large, white-brick pillar that marked the front boundaries of the house. The pillar wasn't going to give an inch, so the car had to. The front end folded up like a paper fan.

It seemed to take forever for the car to settle, as if the trauma happened in slow motion, reverberating from the front to the back of the car in ripples of destruction. The front windshield suddenly seemed to ice over with lethal bits of glassy frost. Then the side windows exploded.

The front driver's door wrenched open, as if the car wanted to expel its contents. Metal buckled hideously. Small pieces, like hubcaps and mirrors, skipped and ricocheted insanely across the oyster-shell driveway.

Finally, everything was still. Into the silence, a plume of steam shot up like a geyser, smelling of rust and heat. Its snake-like hiss almost smothered the low, agonized moan of the driver.

Chase's anger had disappeared. He didn't feel anything but a dull sense of disbelief. Things like this didn't happen in real life. Not in his life. Maybe the sun had actually put him to sleep....

But he was already kneeling beside the car. The

driver was a woman. The frosty glass-ice of the windshield was dotted with small flecks of blood. She must have hit it with her head, because just below her hairline a red liquid was seeping out. He touched it. He tried to wipe it away before it reached her eyebrow, though, of course that made no sense at all. Her eyes were shut.

Was she conscious? Did he dare move her? Her dress was covered in glass, and the metal of the car was sticking out lethally in all the wrong places.

Then he remembered, with an intense relief, that every good medical man in the county was here, just behind the house, drinking his champagne. He found his phone and paged Trent.

The woman moaned again.

Alive, then. Thank God for that.

He saw Trent coming toward him, starting out at a lope, but quickly switching to a full run.

"Get Dr. Marchant," Chase called. "Don't bother with 911."

Trent didn't take long to assess the situation. A fraction of a second, and he began pulling out his cell phone and running toward the house.

The yelling seemed to have roused the woman. She opened her eyes. They were blue and clouded with pain and confusion.

"Chase," she said.

His breath stalled. His head pulled back. "What?"

Her only answer was another moan, and he wondered if he had imagined the word. He reached around her and put his arm behind her shoulders. She was tiny. Probably petite by nature, but surely way too thin. He could feel her shoulder blades pushing against her skin, as fragile as the wishbone in a turkey.

She seemed to have passed out, so he put his other arm under her knees and lifted her out. He tried to avoid the jagged metal, but her skirt caught on a piece and the tearing sound seemed to wake her again.

"No," she said. "Please."

"I'm just trying to help," he said. "It's going to be all right."

She seemed profoundly distressed. She wriggled in his arms, and she was so weak, like a broken bird. It made him feel too big and brutish. And intrusive. As if touching her this way, his bare hands against the warm skin behind her knees, were somehow a transgression.

He wished he could be more delicate. But he smelled gasoline, and he knew it wasn't safe to leave her here.

Finally he heard the sound of voices, as guests began to run around the side of the house, alerted by Trent. Dr. Marchant was at the front, racing toward them as if he were forty instead of seventy. Susannah was right behind him, her green dress floating around her trim legs.

"Please," the woman in his arms murmured again. She looked at him, the expression in her blue eyes lost and bewildered. He wondered if she might be on drugs. Hitting her head on the windshield might account for this unfocused, glazed look, but it couldn't explain the crazy driving.

"Please, put me down. Susannah… The wedding…"

Chase's arms tightened instinctively, and he froze in his tracks. She whimpered, and he realized he might be hurting her. "Say that again?"

"The wedding. I have to stop it."

* * * * *

Be sure to look for TEXAS BABY,
available September 11, 2007,
as well as other fantastic Superromance titles
available in September.

ATHENA FORCE

Heart-pounding romance and thrilling adventure.

Professional negotiator Lindsey Novak is faced with her biggest challenge—to buy back Teal Arnett, a young woman with unique powers. In the process Lindsey uncovers a devastating plot that involves scientists from around the globe, and all of them lead to one woman who is bent on destroying Athena Academy...at any cost.

LOOK FOR

THE GOOD THIEF

by Judith Leon

Available September wherever you buy books.

AF38973

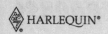

HARLEQUIN®

EVERLASTING LOVE™

Every great love has a story to tell™

Third time's a charm.

Texas summers. Charlie Morrison.
Jasmine Boudreaux has always connected
the two. Her relationship with Charlie
begins and ends in high school. Twenty
years later it begins again—and ends again.
Now fate has stepped in one more time—
will Jazzy and Charlie finally give in to
the love they've shared all this time?

Look for

Summer After Summer
by
Ann DeFee

**Available September
wherever books are sold.**

www.eHarlequin.com

HESAS0907

REQUEST YOUR FREE BOOKS!
2 FREE NOVELS PLUS 2
FREE GIFTS!

HARLEQUIN ROMANCE®

From the Heart, For the Heart

YES! Please send me 2 FREE Harlequin Romance® novels and my 2 FREE gifts. After receiving them, if I don't wish to receive any more books, I can return the shipping statement marked "cancel." If I don't cancel, I will receive 4 brand-new novels every month and be billed just $3.57 per book in the U.S., or $4.05 per book in Canada, plus 25¢ shipping and handling per book and applicable taxes, if any*. That's a savings of over 15% off the cover price! I understand that accepting the 2 free books and gifts places me under no obligation to buy anything. I can always return a shipment and cancel at any time. Even if I never buy another book from Harlequin, the two free books and gifts are mine to keep forever.   114 HDN EEV7 314 HDN EEWK

Name	(PLEASE PRINT)

Address	Apt.

City	State/Prov.	Zip/Postal Code

Signature (if under 18, a parent or guardian must sign)

Mail to the **Harlequin Reader Service®**:
IN U.S.A.: P.O. Box 1867, Buffalo, NY 14240-1867
IN CANADA: P.O. Box 609, Fort Erie, Ontario L2A 5X3

Not valid to current Harlequin Romance subscribers.

Want to try two free books from another line?
Call 1-800-873-8635 or visit www.morefreebooks.com.

* Terms and prices subject to change without notice. NY residents add applicable sales tax. Canadian residents will be charged applicable provincial taxes and GST. This offer is limited to one order per household. All orders subject to approval. Credit or debit balances in a customer's account(s) may be offset by any other outstanding balance owed by or to the customer. Please allow 4 to 6 weeks for delivery.

Your Privacy: Harlequin is committed to protecting your privacy. Our Privacy Policy is available online at www.eHarlequin.com or upon request from the Reader Service. From time to time we make our lists of customers available to reputable firms who may have a product or service of interest to you. If you would prefer we not share your name and address, please check here. ☐

HR07

Coming Next Month

#3973 PROMOTED: NANNY TO WIFE Margaret Way

When dark, brooding Holt McMaster hires Marissa Devlin to be his daughter's new governess, Marissa's heart is quickly stolen by Holt's little girl...and by the magnificent cattle baron himself! Is it possible that the new nanny may also be the perfect wife?

#3974 THE BRIDAL CONTRACT Susan Fox
Western Weddings

Fay Sheridan is facing the bleakest moment of her life, but one man plucks her from despair and into safety...Chase Rafferty. Rugged rancher Chase knows that there is a fun-loving young woman hiding inside Fay, and he will do anything to see her start living again...even propose!

#3975 OUTBACK BOSS, CITY BRIDE Jessica Hart
Bridegroom Boss

Meredith has been forced to take a job on an Outback station with Hal Granger—a boss she can't stand! It should be easy to keep everything purely professional—except she can't stop thinking about what it would be like to kiss him! And Meredith's about to find out....

#3976 NEEDED: HER MR. RIGHT Barbara Hannay
Secrets We Keep

Simone is determined to deal with a dreadful secret she has kept, and move on with her life. Until her private diary is lost...and found by billionaire journalist Ryan Tanner. Simone is immediately suspicious of gorgeous Ryan, but he may just be her Mr. Right in a million....

#3977 THE ITALIAN SINGLE DAD Jennie Adams

Luchino Montichelli broke Bella's heart. Years on he has turned up in Australia with his young daughter. The brooding man who looks at his little girl with such tenderness is the Luc Bella fell in love with. But can she trust him enough to take another chance on this Italian single dad?

#3978 MARRIAGE AT CIRCLE M Donna Alward
Heart to Heart

Town sweetheart Grace Lundquist is determined to hide her pain. But try as she might to keep protective rancher Mike out of her business, Grace can't douse the spark between them. Except she will never be able to give him the one thing he really needs—a family to call his own....